PENGUIN BOOK

ACCESS
ROAD

Maurice Gee is one of New Zealand's best known writers, for both adults and children. He has won a number of literary awards, including the Wattie Award, the Deutz Medal for Fiction and the New Zealand Fiction Award. He has also won the New Zealand Children's Book of the Year Award. In 2003 he received an inaugural New Zealand Icon Award and in 2004 he received a Prime Minister's Award for Literary Achievement.

Maurice Gee's novels include the *Plumb* trilogy, *Going West*, *Prowlers*, *Live Bodies* and *The Scornful Moon*. He has also written a number of children's novels, the most recent being *Salt* and *Gool*.

Maurice lives in Nelson with his wife Margareta, and has two daughters and a son.

ACCESS
ROAD

MAURICE GEE

PENGUIN BOOKS

PENGUIN BOOKS

Published by the Penguin Group

Penguin Group (NZ), 67 Apollo Drive, Rosedale,
North Shore 0632, New Zealand (a division of Pearson New Zealand Ltd)
Penguin Group (USA) Inc., 375 Hudson Street,
New York, New York 10014, USA
Penguin Group (Canada), 90 Eglinton Avenue East, Suite 700, Toronto,
Ontario, M4P 2Y3, Canada (a division of Pearson Penguin Canada Inc.)
Penguin Books Ltd, 80 Strand, London, WC2R 0RL, England
Penguin Ireland, 25 St Stephen's Green,
Dublin 2, Ireland (a division of Penguin Books Ltd)
Penguin Group (Australia), 250 Camberwell Road, Camberwell,
Victoria 3124, Australia (a division of Pearson Australia Group Pty Ltd)
Penguin Books India Pvt Ltd, 11, Community Centre,
Panchsheel Park, New Delhi – 110 017, India
Penguin Books (South Africa) (Pty) Ltd, 24 Sturdee Avenue,
Rosebank, Johannesburg 2196, South Africa

Penguin Books Ltd, Registered Offices: 80 Strand, London, WC2R 0RL, England

First published by Penguin Group (NZ), 2009
1 3 5 7 9 10 8 6 4 2

Copyright © Maurice Gee, 2009

The right of Maurice Gee to be identified as the author of this work in terms of
section 96 of the Copyright Act 1994 is hereby asserted.

Designed by Mary Egan and typeset by Pindar NZ
Printed in Australia by McPherson's Printing Group

ISBN 978 0 14 320244 8

A catalogue record for this book is available
from the National Library of New Zealand.

www.penguin.co.nz

This end of the road novel is for
Margareta, Emily, Abigail, Nigel and
my brothers Aynsley and Gary.

ACKNOWLEDGEMENTS

The story 'Mother's Holiday' on pages 115–120 and the two lines of
poetry on page 125 are by Lyndahl Chapple Gee (1907–1981).

After a long and happy collaboration I'd like to thank my publisher at
Penguin Books, Geoff Walker; my agent, Ray Richards; and especially
my editor, Jane Parkin, for her many improvements to my novels.

one

ONLY DICKIE COULD FALL FROM THE GEOGRAPHICAL
centre of the house and end up in the cactus garden. I was in
bed reading Georgette Heyer when I heard him come in the
front door and pant his way upwards. He stopped at the top
of the stairs to heave a sigh, then his feet drummed backwards
and the landing window exploded. I ran down in my nightie,
put my head through the hole he'd made and saw him lying
crucified in the upturned pots.

'You fool, Dickie, you've done it now,' I cried.

Blood shone like toffee on his face, and his drinker's belly seemed deflated. Yet he opened one eye and tried to smile: 'Care to join me.'

'Oh, shut up,' I said; and said it again, after struggling with the door and picking barefooted through knives of glass and toads of cactus.

He was rolling his head as though searching for something: 'Somebody shifted the top step.'

He's not accident prone, he's a boozer. And he's not stupid, just extravagant. Later, after I'd pulled on my coat and slippers and ferried him to the hospital and had him handed back to me, stitched as neatly as a torn shirt, and he had downed a snort 'to settle his nerves' – but he's nerveless, Dickie – and we were lying in our beds (Georgette trodden under his hoof), he fell to boasting, making a story of it, as I'd known he would.

'Leaned back for the light switch, Boatie, and tangled me feet and did two whole somersaults before I hit the landing. I must've bounced like a tennis ball straight through the bloody glass, how about that? Then six foot down on to the cactus shelves, broke me fall and you know what? There's not a prickle in me. I'm too tough.'

'Just thirty-nine stitches,' I said. 'Now be quiet and go to sleep. No, stay in your own bed. I'll punch you if you come near me.'

He groaned and fell back, and I said, 'Serves you right.' He had bruised his hip and grazed his elbows, and had a glass-cut shaped like a smile in his calf.

I shook one of my precious Zopiclone into his palm and

let him wash it down with whisky, which I shouldn't have, but what the hell. He's seventy-nine, I'm seventy-eight. We've agreed on it: What the hell!

'Thank you, Boatie,' he said meekly.

I'd better explain that name. I'm Rowan Pinker, née Rowan Beach, and when we were young, many years ago, and Dickie was making love to me, he used to joke that he was Rowan his boat – hence Boatie, by degrees. It was a name I wore with secret delight; then for years I hated it and banned it from our vocabulary. Now I quite like it on occasions.

'Go to sleep, Dickie. You've done enough for one night.'

I wrapped a towel around his pillow to soak up the blood. It looked like a butcher's apron in the morning. And rumpled old Dickie could hardly move. He was one purple bruise, and he deserved it.

I let him lie a while, let him inch his way to the toilet and back; then propped him up and brought him breakfast on a tray. I could have given him muesli – 'fowl mash' – but softened sufficiently for porridge, cream, brown sugar and a dob of strawberry jam, and gave him his favourite compliment: 'You stupid old git.' When he had finished I carried in, like a surprise in my clenched hand, Cartia, Lipex, Betaloc, and waited to make sure he swallowed them.

I don't want Dickie dead yet. I want to go first. 'What the hell!' is the starter's call in a race. He hears it too – and yet I ask, how does all this jokiness and toughness sit with love? He doesn't ask the question; he's having too much fun – but

I think of his tenderness and care when I'm sick: putting cold flannels on my brow, tucking me in and kissing me goodnight. I do the same for him, and sponge his wounds and change his mucky dressings. It's love of a sort, our invention, behind which no anxiety lurks – although I'd better speak just for myself. It hasn't got the freshness and delight of our first years, but ease and humour in their place, and a wonderful absence of the bitterness in me and cruelty in him that made a wasteland of our middle years.

I won't go there, and when I do, if I must, I won't hang around.

In the meantime, Cheryl came. She wanted to laugh and wanted to cry, and studied him with leaking eyes that soon needed repairing. She threw off her linen jacket to stop blood getting on it, and knelt like Mary Magdalene and took him in her arms. When she detached there was red on her blouse. She pulled the cloth away from her skin, making a sound of disgust, then hugged him again. Such love! I get no look in, although the dear girl – dear woman of fifty – lies at the centre of my heart.

I did not want a Cheryl, but agreed, to save her from worse – candyfloss names, euphonic horrors, were coming in. I wanted Helen. Dickie won the fight and our daughter grew up satisfied with her pretty name. Now she's a much-loved stranger, intimately known and not understood. Busy-busy with her job, and busy with an activity she calls dating, pronouncing that juvenile term with assurance. Divorced from her husband, dislocated (her term) from several partners, still she tries. She's full of experience and not in the least surprised by failing love, but cries like a teenager at betrayal. At the moment she's without a live-in partner and so has time for Dickie and me, and for trans-Tasman interference in her sons' lives. (Rufus is in Sydney and Simon in Perth, where he has ambitions to get even further away.)

When Dickie started boasting about his fall – practising the story he'd tell at his club – and Cheryl responded with cross exclamations and grins of delight, I excused myself and phoned our handyman to clean up the glass. I pulled on my gardening gloves and stepped among the wreckage – scimitars and sheets of ice and diamonds and tears – picking up my cactus plants and lining them up along the patio wall. I don't much like cactuses. They're a test. Can I make these things that hate me reward my perseverance with a flower? Can I coax out beauty from those spines and fists? And cactuses are part of my conversation – call it a game – with Dickie, who's a rose man.

Roses ambushed him. When we bought this house, they were in possession and we made ready to pull them out, but spring came along and the buds burst out, delighting us with their complexity, simplicity, colours, perfume, their tenderness and boldness and profusion. Mine, I said. I wanted them. Mine, said Dickie, more slowly and with puzzlement, but with a rounder view soon reinforced by knowledge. He knows aphids, he knows black spot – he carries a rose gun –

and mulching and pruning, all those things. Roses are not a test with him as cactuses are with me, they're a contest. He plays fair and steady all season – plays hard too, against what he calls the best defensive system in nature – and wins with an array of perfect blooms. Dickie sheds blood for his roses. He won't wear gardening gloves, likes to give the thorns a crack at him. They jag and scratch his hands and arms and sometimes his face; they fester and sting; but Dickie earns another unfolding. I've seen him hold a full-blown rose in his hands like a child's face. He buries his torn cheeks in the petals and drinks the perfume. It's a consummation.

These are some of the things that make me put up with Dickie Pinker; and putting-up-with, at my time of life, is only a nudge away from love.

BUT ROSES DON'T COME FIRST IN HIS LIFE. CHERYL AND I come first; it's a dead heat. Then comes his club. Then bowls. Then rugby. Rufus and Simon don't make the list – they're a generation too far. He's not even interested in what they're doing, and when he senses failure in this sends them presents of money. I'm sure they prefer it to Dickie's attention.

My brothers, Lionel and Roly, come nowhere. But I'll leave Lionel and Roly for later on.

Griff, our handyman, arrived (Dickie gets on first-name terms with everyone who knocks.) He cleaned up the broken glass and set up my cactus stands again, then phoned a glazier.

Dickie had Cheryl call Griff upstairs for a wee nip, which she made sure was 'wee', and watered down too. She and I walked on the beach. The tide lay half out. A spring breeze rippled the sea and brought up goose-bumps on Cheryl's arms, which she folded on her chest to hide her blood-stained blouse. She was wearing shoes awkward for sand-walking, so we found a place to sit on a stone wall.

'Don't you let him go to the club,' she said.

'Do you really think I can stop him?'

'You should put your foot down, Mum. I would. I'd . . .' Dickie, his intransigence, was too strong in her mind for the sentence to go anywhere. She lit a cigarette instead, and stubbed it out after a puff because she's given up.

'He could have been killed.'

I did not say what I thought: that heart attack or stroke could whack him like a hammer any day. Observed instead that all of us can be killed at any old time – to which she answered angrily, 'Oh, Mum.' Then, re-hearing my remark, shot a look at me and held it steady: 'Are you all right?'

'Yes, I'm fine.' No health worries to speak of, no death worries, just intermittent stress, which is no stress at all, and sleepless nights, and brothers and a husband, and a daughter whose unhappiness makes me unhappy. She's happy now, though, because there's a new man in the offing. She sold him an apartment, after warning him of traffic noise, which she wasn't obliged to do. He's a little deaf, so it doesn't matter; and he appreciates her honesty. He has asked her in for drinks –

my pretty, hopeful, sweet-smelling daughter. I hope . . . Those words, those stops, make a diagram of where I'm at.

We scurried back along the beach in front of the rising wind. Dickie and Griff were on their second Black. (Dickie has two drinks: Johnny Walker Black Label, and a malt with an unpronounceable name for special occasions. Both are ugly brews as far as I'm concerned. I sip sherry, very dry.) I sent our handyman away with what my mother would have called a flea in his ear. I sent Cheryl away, after lending her a blouse so her blood stains wouldn't scare the rich American she was showing a cliff-top house to in Torbay.

Dickie was tired, he was groggy, he was hurting. I put him to sleep with Panadeine and told the glazier to be as quiet as he could. Then I lay down on the chaise longue in the lounge, and slept a little and dreamed unpleasantly. I'm dogged by anxiety dreams, and this time there was a long way to go and no time left and I was still in my nightie. Then I was in the car, which was rolling backwards down a hill towards the sea no matter how hard I stood on the brake. I woke with a start and found the sun on my face, and my foot – the brake foot – numb, and heard Dickie calling my name. He had been dreaming too. His dream was that I'd left him.

'Fat chance,' I said, stroking the half dozen hairs off his brow.

So the day went on, and the next, and the next. I've put aside 'What the hell' until his stitches are out.

His friends came in and he entertained them. They drank

cups of tea – even that loosely tied parcel of appetites, Ron Stock. Dickie improved his story. His number of stitches grew. I found the process interesting. His was a drunkard's fall. Looseness, mental as well as physical, saved him, but he inserted quickness and intention – a shoulder at the glass to drive the falling blades away, a forearm guarding his throat to save his jugular. What would he invent next? I'm reminded that he played rugby for Auckland – I used to watch him – and that he was 'nearly an All Black'. (The number of 'nearly' All Blacks I've met!) I'm familiar with the stories of his best tries, the men he beat with a change of pace or a dummy, his dive for the corner; and now he's diving into the cactus garden. That's all right. But I won't let Ron Stock get away with his smug assumption that he knows Dickie better than I. They were business partners, no more than that. I ordered him out when I caught him tipping whisky from his monogrammed hip-flask into Dickie's tea; and might have bumped him accidentally at the top of the stairs if the painter hadn't been busy with an undercoat on the new window surrounds.

THIS AFTERNOON, AFTER A WEEK IN WHICH 'WHAT THE hell' has been on hold, Dickie is at his club again. His stitches don't come out for another few days, and I'm anxious for that – anxious for a return to our non-anxiety. I haven't enjoyed holding him in check. But I was pleased to see him stop in the rose garden as he left and wipe out a colony of aphids with his thumb. Yellow-thumbed, he was off up the road without a backward glance – dear Dickie Pinker, whom I loved once, and almost hated once, and now almost love again. I watched him out of sight, then walked on the beach – firm sand, small waves, a pale inverted sky. I reached the far end and strode home happy. A cup of tea, a clean page: I attempted a poem, which curled up and died on line two for want of a rhyme. Never mind. Poetry is written by poets and most of them don't bother with rhyming any more. I wish I understood that. I once rhymed Pinker with stinker. I rhymed Dick with prick. And the boys at Loomis School mis-rhymed Beach with bitch: 'Rowan Beach is a skinny bitch.' I was thin in those days (I'm lean now). I had legs like a racehorse and won all the running races at the school sports.

Memories serve me better than poetry.

For my dinner I fried gurnard fillets in butter and boiled the first asparagus of the season. I ate off a tray, watching the TV news, and saw policemen dressed like storm-troopers throw tear-gas canisters through the window of a house in Loomis. It was not my brothers' house, not their street (my street). It would take more than tear gas to get Lionel out of bed. But two old men living together like Lionel and Roly might very well stage a 'domestic incident'.

I put my tray aside and telephoned them, but as usual nobody answered. Lionel won't, and Roly is in the garden as long as the light lasts, which now we're into daylight saving is close to eight o'clock. I don't worry about them. I've stopped that. When I think of them, it's fondly, as a rule, and then I become retrogressive, deeply retrogressive, and so much enjoy it that sometimes hours will go by before I spring back into Takapuna, Dickie, and dishes in the sink and the vacuuming to be done. Where have I been? What have I seen?

A muddy street, a clay bank, a little weatherboard house with a leadlight window in the front wall. The evening sun strikes through a rose with blood-red petals and pea-green leaves and makes opposing handprints on my bedroom door. Out in the twilight Roly carves a mountain road in the clay bank and drives his Dinky car along it. Lionel throws his sheath knife at a piece of cardboard tacked to the pine tree in the top corner of the section. He takes no notice of our mother calling him. Dad gets his razor strop from the bathroom and whacks it on the tank stand – a crack like a gunshot that brings Lionel skulking in with his knife in its sheath. Roly hears it too and comes running. Both have muddy feet, and our mother sends them into the wash-house to sit in the tubs and get every bit of mud out from between their toes before she'll allow them in the kitchen. Lionel has stubbed his big toe. The flap of skin opens like a cupboard door. She paints it with iodine, which makes him yelp, and bandages it with a strip of rag torn off a shirt. Then we sit down to eat – and what meal shall I choose? A mince-meat stew with boiled cabbage and boiled potatoes? I hated it then and love the memory now: the grey mince, the soggy cabbage like a pale green cowpat, the potatoes like cakes of soap. And yet, like my brothers, I gobbled it, and mightn't it be closer to the truth to say that I hate it now and loved it then? I was no soft, superior girl. I came in hungry after climbing trees and crawling through culverts and throwing Lionel's sheath knife at the pine tree when he'd let me. I made it stick in a few times. I can't remember ever refusing food. My favourite was a beef stew made from rag-end meat – lots of fat – and, if we were lucky, a doughboy on top. How did I stay skinny after that? There were sausages fried and sausages curried and sausages baked in a batter pie. There was rice pudding and sago pudding and custard. Bread pudding too, I didn't mind that. We ate cheap food and plenty of vegetables – silverbeet, curly kale, runner beans, butter beans out of Dad's garden . . . How memory drifts from people to things and back again, and on to events, and out to places, out to landscapes – the faraway hills – and lifts away layers of inconsequence and melts the years to nothing like the morning sun with a fog . . .

Memory leaves me with clammy sticks of asparagus and cold gurnard fillets. It interferes with Georgette when I settle in the corner of the sofa to read. It's like that with me. Loomis builds into an imperative. I must take time away from Dickie Pinker. He can manage for an afternoon. Tomorrow I'll commandeer the car and drive into the west, towards those hills far away, and find Access Road, where my brothers wait, silent, gruff and dirty, in the little house where I grew up.

two

THE HOUSES THAT I KNEW ARE STILL THERE, BUT NOW others squeeze in beside them. It's called infill, although infill was a second stage after the gorse and scrub sections on the high side of the street were cleared and planted with spec houses in the fifties. By that time the street had been pushed through Dawson's farm to meet the Great North Road and was blind no longer. I don't know when it was sealed and framed in concrete footpaths, but as I drive down the gentle slope my forebrain grows dizzy with possession and my throat aches with loss.

Along at our end, the former railway houses opposite the Beach house sit undisturbed. There are five of them – red roofs, a green roof, a blue roof, weatherboards in pastel shades, except for one (the McEvoy house when I was a girl) in a terminal condition, with rusty iron, curling paint and rotten window frames.

Our house is on the upper side, the better side, with front windows looking out to the Waitakere Ranges – a view that once had a middle ground of farms and orchards and vineyards but now takes in the new metropolis, Waitakere City. There seems to be nowhere the shops and warehouses haven't gone, and I have learned the trick of nullifying everything that lies out there and recreating, in a kind of 'let there be', the green paddocks and round-headed trees and faraway blue bush of my girlhood, when Dad and Mum owned our house and Lionel and Roly were boys with scabby knees and Rowan Beach their knowing sister.

Dad sold the house in 1947. Lionel bought it back in 1983. He lived there alone until Roly joined him as the century was turning. I've watched them like a pair of fish in a bowl. I visit them when I can muster the energy and when I calculate that love won't be overcome by revulsion. Is it love? I don't know. When I drive out from Takapuna and down past the mangroves to the harbour bridge, I need to be in that state of good humour that tips, by a natural progression, into more of itself and works like a masseur's palpating fingers, promoting laziness, promoting affection.

I go through Herne Bay and Westmere and get on the motorway at Point Chevalier; scurry north – I'm a scurrying driver, even in Dickie's giant Volvo – to Lincoln Road, and turn towards Loomis; and good humour survives this roundabout approach because I know that soon I'll be crossing Loomis Creek, although without a glimpse of its murky water, and climbing the hill past Loomis School. The old four-roomed building, high shouldered, narrow eyed, stands like a pensioner among new-built classrooms in pretty dresses – classrooms with low foreheads, I say – and it brings a hailstorm of memories, never fails, and I say, 'Ha' and I say, 'Yes' and I say, 'No'. ('No,' with disbelief and embarrassment, 'did I do that?')

I'm a dangerous driver the rest of the way up the hill, but there are no lights to negotiate, only a turn across the traffic. I manage it and I'm in Access Road, where school memories flick away like sheets of paper in a storm and I become hard-minded and critical, for this end isn't mine and has no authenticity. Mine, Access Road, is the other end, and even there it's only a small part held like a nut in a hard shell: the Beach house with its left-side neighbour, the Meikle house, and the Wiggins on its other side, and the five railway houses over the street. As for the rest, among the infill, and the lost swamp and abandoned orchard and the slopes of gorse tangled like wire, and the two culverts and Kelly's farm and the draught-horse paddock sloping down to the creek, they are like the fibrous casing that lies around the hard shell of some nuts – but now I'm pushing it too far. There are judgements to be made and anger to be coped with – that shock of anger that someone, thirty years ago, painted our house blue. Our house is white. The Beach house is white, eternally.

The lawns are mown, there's not a weed in sight. The hedge is clipped, and the clay bank, once carved with roads for Roly's Dinky toys, is a hanging carpet of groundcover, yellow and green, housing, no doubt, a million insects – lucky things to be living in such comfort there. This is Roly's work, Roly the gardener.

A nurseryman had owned the property before Lionel bought it back. He had resisted infill, resisted the blandishments of developers, and built two medium-sized glasshouses at the back of the section, where he grew tomatoes, courgettes, melons, and raised seedlings of all sorts. Lionel had no interest in that. Growth made him suspicious, perhaps afraid. He let the section turn into a jungle, which must have increased his fear. Jungle at the front and back; jungle inside the glasshouses, which burst their roofs and pushed out their walls and planted glittering teeth among the dock and thistle and the crazy vegetables busily converting into weeds. So it went on until Roly came. The Beach section grew famous as an eyesore and exemplar of neglect. All that time Lionel stayed inside. He's inside now, in his room, in his bed.

Roly arrived eight years ago. He walked in, touched nothing in the house, just made himself a place to cook and a place to sleep. He set to work on the section and has done all this: the groundcover, the hedges, the lawns at the front, the multi-leaved, multi-fruited garden running to the macrocarpa hedge at the back, squared along the boundary with the Catholic school. The glasshouses are gone, their wreckage gone. Tons of glass were carted away. There's a garden shed between a nectarine tree and a peach tree. There's a compost bin – it's more: a compost set of apartments where magical transformations take place – a worm farm and drums of liquid manure. Everything is wholesome and clean; decay is clean, putrefaction is turned to use. And the vegetables grow. Do you want to see silverbeet the way silverbeet should be, so glossy green it hurts the eyes; and pumpkins, carrots, potatoes, oh potatoes, kumara . . .? Roly's garden takes my breath away. I'm scarcely able to believe that one old man digging with a shovel (he uses a shovel, not a spade), scraping with a hoe, his trousers held up with a cast-off tie, has made all this.

When he had sent the rubbish away in half a dozen truckloads, leaving the old dunny to house his tools, Roly dug the back of the section by hand. The property is a full quarter acre (I can't do hectares) and that makes the garden an eighth. He turned up a dozen old dumps of cans and bottles, some dating from the Beaches' first occupation (Roly is a canny chap: he sold the bottles to collectors). Each sod received a whack on the back of its head with the shovel. The soil was friable and soon gave the appearance of a choppy sea at full tide. When the last square inch was turned to his satisfaction, Roly said, 'Now then,' like Micky Savage. I had no idea of the labour 'Now then' heralded. I went away and left him to it, pleased that he was occupied and that Lionel had his brother to keep an eye on him.

Eight years later, here's the garden, and here they are, two old men sharing a house, one of them ruling inside and the other absolute monarch of the section.

LIONEL RULES BY NEGATIVE INFLUENCE. HIS BED IS jammed against the wall like a bench in a changing shed. There's no need to look for him anywhere else except the toilet. He won't accept Roly's help or mine in freeing him from his blankets and getting him there. Several months ago Roly set up a bell for him to ring. A rope runs on pulleys through the ceiling cavity. The bell hangs over the back door, like the one that signalled playtime at Loomis School, but although Lionel was bell-ringer in standard six and Roly cajoles him with the memory, he refuses to touch the rope dangling by his hand. Roly gives it a jerk now and then. 'Just testing,' he says. He's pleased with his contraption.

He was working in the tomatoes when I arrived. His roadman's shovel stood upright in the soil with his hat sitting on top – one of those thirties hats creased lengthwise in the crown. I'm surprised there are any left; but if Roly has an image of himself it's as a workman, and the hat fits, although when the sun gets too hot he wears a knotted handkerchief instead.

'How is he?' I called.

'Same,' Roly said.

'I'll make a cup of tea soon.'

'Ring the bell.'

I stepped inside. Now there's a journey. I was dizzy again as I walked crookedly through the house, calling 'Lionel' to warn him I was coming. I crossed the narrow kitchen, passing the cavity that once housed our old wood range. The rose window bloomed as I entered the sitting room. It made red and green puddles on the floor, where the carpet, worn along a track to Lionel's bedroom door, raised loops of string to catch my feet.

'Lionel,' I said, 'you've got to get some mats before someone breaks his neck.'

Wherever he travels in his mind, there are things that won't let him go. I had crossed the room and lowered myself into the bedside chair before he was able to free himself. He moved his head 30 degrees on the pillow, opened his eyes wider, 30 degrees, and found me.

'You,' he said.

'Yes, me, Lionel. Me again. I'm your sister and I need to know how you are.'

'Sister blister,' he said.

'That's not very nice.'

Our conversations go this way. I'm happy as long as words are coming out. Mine rise from affection and sorrow, no matter how worn and formulaic they sound; his from the denizen inhabiting his skull. What is that creature? Why, it's Lionel of course. Unless you believe in demons taking possession, there's no way to deny that connection. Here is Lionel; Lionel dying. This is my brother with the scabby knees. He, in that and every subsequent manifestation, is householder, denizen, monarch there, and is subject to himself.

I took out my chapstick and oiled my lips. 'How are you, Lionel?'

He turned his head away the same distance, closed his eyes, then opened them. It was like changing gears in a car.

'You don't need to come,' he said.

'I like coming. I want to come.'

Long pause, while my words wound through the half-blocked channels of his consciousness.

Do I fail in love by expressing things so? I'm simply trying to understand. Past and present, good and bad, pain and pleasure, success, failure, obsession, prejudice, and all his acts of commission and omission thicken and spit inside his bony skull. I hear them with a sense beyond normal hearing and know their provenance in his life and mine. Yet there is something I don't know. I've given up hope of discovering it. He'll never make admissions. Reluctance sets in him like tar. And why shouldn't it? He's dying and it takes all his time.

'Let me help you outside. I'll put a chair in the sun.'

When he makes no movement, doesn't even blink his eyes, he's saying no.

'It's a lovely day. You can watch Roly pinching his laterals.'

He whispered something. Was it 'laterals'? The word had a flavour for him. He closed his eyes on it, and I sat quiet while he did whatever he does with a new idea – processed it. I used the time to map his face, crown to jaw, then went further, to his turkey throat, where the singlet under his pyjama top looped its grey hem round his Adam's apple. Lionel is growing warts in his hairline and soft little bulbs of aberrant skin on his cheeks. His eyes leak, his nose leaks, while his lips, when he draws them back, as he often does, reveal his beautifully shaped but now discoloured acrylic crowns.

People say you should be able to find the boy in the man. I can't find Lionel, no matter how hard I try. But shouldn't I want this person now, the one in the bed, rather than that person there?

After a while he said, 'You can go away now.'

I replied, 'Do you remember . . . ?'

That is the way we converse. He orders me out; I sit tight, while retreating from my ambition to know the man, and remind him of things that happened when we were young.

'Do you remember the fancy-dress concert in the Loomis town hall? You were the king in his counting house, counting out his money. You were wearing your pyjamas, and a dressing gown Mum made from one of Dad's old shirts. Joan Tribe was the queen, eating bread and honey. You recited on the stage, remember . . .'

That is the way I go on.

'Down flew a blackbird and pecked off her nose – that's Dulcie Fountain's nose. She was the maid. But who was the blackbird? I can't remember. Dulcie cried because the elastic sprang back and whacked her in the mouth.'

Lionel never responds. I'm a radio droning news from nowhere.

'And then you . . . and then I . . . then Roly . . .' Hearing myself, I understand his deafness. But how else am I to fill half an hour sitting by Lionel's bed?

Halfway through the fancy-dress concert, he stopped me by turning his head. I'm never sure what his eyes see, not sure that if I bend to look I'll find myself mirrored there. His focus stops short of other people – of the four he sees: Roly, me, his doctor, his once-a-week carer who washes him. He lifted his hands from the coverlet and mimed – such minimal acting: a flattening of one hand, a finger placed on the palm like a pencil.

'Pencil? Paper? You want to write?'

I found them on the table by his bed, a biro not a pencil, and a land agent's gift pad with a prettied-up woman smirking at the bottom of the page (so agents were pestering again). I placed them in Lionel's hands, half-believing he had a message for me, and watched as he wrote.

One word. *Lateral*. That was all. Tiny letters, neat and square, made with his drill hand.

Lionel doesn't shake or twitch. Except for occasional necessary uses, his body doesn't seem part of him any more. All his life is in his head – in that head ruined by age and illness, which I can't force into conjunction with dentistry. Lionel bending close to peer into the wet pink cavity of a mouth? Never. No.

Yet that was how Lionel, handsome faced, spent his working life. He worked in a practice in Christchurch, then part-owned one in Loomis. He sold his share in 1983 and bought our old Access Road house. He moved in and scarcely came into the open air again.

He held the pad and biro until I took them from his hands.

'Do you want to go and see Roly's tomatoes, is that it?'

I knew very well it was not, but conversation is hard to make when it's so one-sided and I take every opening I can get. I might do better sitting quiet, but that's even harder.

'Do you remember Mr Drummond's tomatoes, when you and Roly raided them and used them in a fight? One of them hit Mr Finn's car coming up the road. That wasn't the worst hiding Dad ever gave you. That was the Catholic school.'

Lionel closed his eyes. The meaning is, he's closing his ears.

'Go and make Roly a cup of tea,' he whispered.

'And one for you? Just a sip? With plenty of milk?' I pleaded.

A small sideways movement of his head also means no.

I touched his cheek – the only physical comfort I bring – and went into the kitchen, where a fridge not much bigger than a butter box sits on the bench. The milk was full cream, thank heaven. Roly does the shopping every second or third day; walks down the right-of-way by the McEvoy house, crosses the busy road running by the creek, and the wide bridge where once a swing-bridge bounced and swayed, and stalks the aisles in one of the supermarkets in Loomis Mall. I sometimes think he picks at random: instant noodles, chocolate almonds, whole smoked chickens, tomato sauce, bacon, sardines, date scones, flavoured milk. I made his tea with chocolate milk one day, to teach him a lesson. He drank it with no comment.

Our mother worked in this kitchen more than sixty years ago. The lino, old even in her day, has given way to vinyl faked to look like Provençal tiles. The wooden sink bench is replaced with stainless steel, and the electric stove, so exciting when it took the place of our wood stove, has given way to a built-in range with an eye-level oven. The nurseryman did this. Lionel has made no improvements. Roly has none to suggest. He describes the kitchen as 'pretty flash'.

I carried two mugs of tea into the garden and put them on the brick table Roly built last summer beside the dunny. There are two chairs: an old sea-grass recliner painted with enamel to preserve it, and a spindly canvas thing that's going to collapse one day. Roly came, smelling of tomatoes, and took the canvas one. Mum taught her sons to be gentlemen, and in Roly the lesson survives. Item: Roly stands aside at a door to let me through. Item: Roly raises his hat to a lady. I've a dozen more examples but that's enough. He's formal in his behaviour, he's clean in his mind, he still believes ladies don't swear – and if they do they're 'hard boiled'. He thinks I'm hard boiled and blames Dickie. He never mentions Dickie or asks about my life in Takapuna, which he describes as 'an upper-crust place'.

'I didn't get anywhere with him,' I said.

'Nowhere to get,' Roly said.

'There must be. He's got all sorts of things going on in his head. He writes down words.'

'And then forgets them.'

'How do you know?'

Roly cooled his tea with a noisy sucking (a workman, not a gentleman, in his tea-drinking habits). 'Ever heard him use one?' he said.

'That doesn't mean . . .' I did not know what it didn't mean.

Roly lay back in his chair, making the canvas creak and the bolts groan. He sighed with enjoyment; he grinned at the sun.

'Leave him,' he said. 'Hold his hand.'

'Anyone can do that. I'm his sister.'

'Sister blister.'

'He said that.'

'It's the only joke he knows.'

'Stupid.'

'I thought it was pretty good.'

Roly took more long swallows from his mug. When the tea was finished he poked his index finger inside and dug muddy sugar from the bottom. His habits don't bother me. All I want is for him to keep going: work in his garden, look after Lionel, be contented. It's his easiness and contentment that make him likeable. But here's a strange thing. I spent more time with Roly than Lionel when we were young, yet fewer memories attach to him. I liked him more and like him more today. Why then do I hold on to Lionel? Why do I love him even as I shrink from him?

'Has the doctor been?'

'He doesn't like home visits. He reckons Lionel should go to his rooms.'

'That's absurd. He can't.'

'He could if he wanted to. There's nothing wrong with him, Rowan. Only in his head.'

'There's polymyalgia.'

'That won't kill him, it'll only hurt.'

'Is he taking his pills – what are they, Prednisone?'

Roly dug the last sugar out of his mug. He sucked his finger, yellow from pinching laterals.

'He puts them in his pyjama pocket, then flushes them down the toilet.'

'Why? You've got to stop him doing that.'

'Not me. A man's got a right. Lionel wants to feel what he's got.'

'But polymyalgia is like . . . Roly, it hurts.'

'That's what he wants. He wants to hurt.'

'This is mad. I'm telling the doctor.'

'Won't do any good. Anyway, the doctor's not a bad guy. I reckon he thinks if Lionel wants to die it's his own business.'

'No doctor can think that. It's against their oath.'

Roly laughed. 'It'd be a great world if it was simple like that.'

'Is he eating? Is Lionel eating?'

'He likes smoked chicken. Doesn't spit it out.'

'What about greens?' I waved at the silverbeet leaping from the soil.

'Doesn't go for them. Take it easy, Ro. He's in there dying. He'll have his reasons. Leave him alone.'

'There's nothing he's got that will kill him.'

Roly sighed. He tapped his head. 'He's got what's in here.'

'And what's that? What is it?'

'Nothing he'll ever tell us about. Now give it a bone. Things are pretty smooth here –'

'Smooth!'

The worst Roly ever gets is ruffled. He was close to it, but laughed instead, with a rueful patience. 'Nice cup of tea. Now I've got to get my watering started. And you need to beat the four o'clock traffic.'

That is Roly. When he wants to get rid of me, he tells me to beat the traffic – four o'clock, five o'clock, whatever time it is. Roly doesn't own a car.

I washed the mugs in the kitchen, then looked at Lionel again. His hands lay outside the blanket, facing each other like crabs. I picked one of them up and kissed it, because he hates me kissing his face.

'You must take your pills, Lionel. You must.' I put his hand back in its position. 'I'll come again in two or three days. I expect to see you looking better by then.'

Roly met me in the yard with two plastic bags of vegetables, silverbeet and a lettuce in one, carrots and radishes in the other.

'Lovely,' I said. 'But I can't use them all, Roly.'

'Give them away,' he said.

I drove home, beating the four o'clock traffic, and caught Dickie leaving for his club.

Dickie is a huge relief to me. He brings me back into the world.

three

MY FATHER, FRED BEACH, WAS A BOOTMAKER. HE caught the early train at Loomis station and travelled to Mt Eden where he worked at a bench in a factory. He had no ambitions to rise higher or to start out on his own. Mum pointed out to him several times that Loomis had no boot repairer. Dad wouldn't listen. He slid back and forth in his groove. Habit was the oil. His eyes began to jump with fright if Mum kept on at him too long.

Mum brought four hundred and nineteen pounds into the marriage (the sum was family lore), enough to buy the house with some left over. We sat there through the Depression and survived with no rent to pay; then Dad was back on his train, to Mum's disgust. He whistled walking off in the dawn, and whistled coming home. Life was bloody hard but also pretty good. That was the lesson we took from Dad.

From Mum we took sugar, spice and everything nice. We took long views out to where beauty might be found, as well as the habit of examining closer things, things overlooked, where secrets hidden from the common herd might be uncovered. Mum gave an impression of simplicity because she was pure in thought and deed, and because she was superior, which was a plain state although mysterious. Where did she come from? A good Christchurch family where her dad was headmaster of a school and her mother drank tea and visited, and her sisters had married well, that was where. We saw these storied folk being nice to each other like a family in the pictures, sitting down to dinner, patting the dog, pecking each other goodnight on the cheek, plain as day. The mystery was how it connected with us. I thought, I'll find a door and step through when I'm grown up. I thought, One day I'll take Mum back home.

I don't think she regretted what she had lost. It was real; she identified it, and bred small selected pieces into her children's behaviour – good manners, quiet voices, little observances of precedence and obligation, a ceremony of goodnight when we went to bed: things I remember and practise inside myself even as I leave them neglected in word and deed.

She had, she told us, been a rebel, but not in a way that might upset her parents. They did not object to her writing poems and posting them off to the newspaper. She carried out rebellions in her head and planned to slide away, causing no ripple, when the time came, leaving her parents comfortable and unperturbed on the shore. They had other ideas, which they put forward in the shape of a man. 'And he had quite nice eyes,' Mum used to say, 'but he didn't have a single idea in his head.' That did not surprise her – her father had none either, although he had opinions. What she objected to even more in the suitor was that he was fat under his chin and had fat hands. My mother did not understand herself, but there's no doubt she was a sensualist, and for carnal pleasure she required a straight, tall, big-boned man. She could not love any other sort. Along came my father. He too had not a single thought in this head, but for the time of their courtship and nuptials, and for a short while after, it did not matter.

How flowery I'm getting. Courtship. Nuptials. The Christchurch suitor had conducted a courtship (bunches of violets in his fat hands). When it was over, Mum visited an Auckland aunt to enjoy her relief at being quit of him, and there, on a beach (where else in our subtropical city?), met Dad quietly showing off his muscles and his tan. 'Quietly' has importance here. Loudness would have been inexcusable. Poor Dad. His quietness was really a kind of passiveness, hiding his confusion about every next moment in his life. Mum took it for sincerity. She took his difference from her as an opportunity for adventure, and loved, loved with carnal excitement, his long back, wide shoulders, big hands, muscular legs; his shy, sincere, handsome countenance; and gave herself happily to their future. I won't speculate about what they did and where, just remark that Lionel was born several months too soon.

Mum must have felt she had a mouldable lump of clay – Dad, I mean, not the baby. But he put his uncertainties aside like a package he had not known where to lay down. A wife, a child, a house taught him, inside a year, who he was. He was breadwinner, bootmaker, catcher of the morning train and weekend digger in the garden. He was painter of our roof cherry red and our walls icy white. He dug steps down to the road and concreted them. He strung a clothes-line across the back lawn, long enough for sheets and towels and a dozen nappies. How do I know these things? Mum described them with loving care. She hoped for him. She described them with an edge of bitterness too, as though he were a stallion, glossy and beautiful, that had, all the same, lost the race.

Lionel, Rowan, Roland: she chose our names. She meant us to have every advantage. There would be no Bettys or Toms among the Beaches, and no more Freds. (She was Isobel and heaven help anyone who called her Izzy.) So we wore our names to school, where we found a Digby and a Cyril, a Winsome and a Jonquil and a Dulcie. Several of them were ridiculed; and Roly was called Roly-poly now and then. But Lionel was as savage as a fighting dog and as quick to strike as a cat, and nobody took the risk of making fun of him. I could run and scratch and shriek, and Lionel taught me to punch with the knuckle of my middle finger out. As well as that, I was sharp with my tongue so I was high up among the girls who ruled the playground. If the boys teased me, it was because I was pretty and had red hair.

Lionel and Roland were sandy; they had what Mum called man's hair. Mine was rich and full of light, and had a soft unassertive wave. 'Princess hair,' she said, brushing it. She worked hard to make me feel it was special, and after a complaining time when I wanted dark or fair, I began to carry my head as though I wore a crown. But stately didn't suit me, stately was a bore. There was a song on the radio at that time:

> There were ten pretty girls at the village school . . .
> Four were blondes and five brunettes
> And one was a saucy little redhead.

I loved 'saucy'. It became my word, so strong and convincing I simply removed myself with a sideways turn when Lionel tipped tomato sauce on his plate and inquired if anyone else wanted a bit of Rowan. He also teased me with the last lines of the song, which had all the time been less about the pretty girls than the boy who loved them:

> At twenty-one he wedded
> The saucy little redhead.

That part didn't interest me. Saucy was my position, and I took a stance and acquired movements – hip out, then round on my heel and away – and an expression, something between a grin and a simper, that fitted with it. I had a set of sounds too, from giggle to shriek. All this, when I remembered. That wasn't often. I was too busy being unaware and natural, which I mean as praise of myself.

Dad managed the boys. Because his father whipped him, he whipped Lionel and Roly, but not often and not too hard. It was called 'a good hiding', and although Mum pulled me out to the back lawn and covered her ears and made me cover mine, she agreed a lesson of that sort was right for boys. What was right for me was a smack with the back of the hearth brush on my bare bottom, and Mum gave that – while Dad uttered whimpers of distress. He might go out in the dusk and smack his razor strop against the tank stand to bring the boys running; he might, when they had been especially bad, unfold his pocket knife and cut a willow switch from the hedge; he might come home bloody-mouthed from a fight with a fellow worker in the factory yard – but Dad was what is known these days as a softie. He believed in moderation and, even more, in kindness. He was deferential to women, almost chivalric with them. Somewhere in his private thoughts they rode side-saddle on white ponies with chaplets of flowers in their hair. Smacking my bare bottom broke a code.

❖ ❖ ❖

LIONEL'S WILDNESS COULD NOT HAVE BEEN GENETIC. Nor could upbringing have been the cause. In a way, my brother felt the call of the wild.

Our house sat in the middle of a territory. Behind it, through the hedge and past a triangle of waste land, was the Catholic school, with a church for the Loomis faithful and a convent for the nuns. Kelly's farm lay alongside, its back paddocks fenced off from the scrub acre next to our house. Beyond the farm was Burke's orchard, falling into dereliction. A narrow weed-infested creek ran through it, then lost itself in two acres of wiry gorse before reaching the culvert under Access Road. Remembering the culvert, I tell myself, Go through. There's ankle-deep silt and rotting vegetation and maybe eels inside, but if you walk on the curve of the pipe you can sometimes reach the other side dry-footed. The world is an O, then it's a swamp with brown water and sharp rushes and old willow trees that lay out squishy mats of fibrous root – red, like my hair. The swamp widens and gets dangerous. It can suck you down. The last of you anyone will see is hands clutching air. Turn away from it; climb through more gorse into another orchard – this one abandoned, its trees smothered in honeysuckle shaped like wigwams. Here and there a branch pokes out with a withered apple on it. The creek, the big creek, lies beyond – an arrangement of shallows and sharp rapids and deep pools. You can reach it by ploughing through the orchard, but a better way is through the draught-horse paddock at the far end of the railway houses. That is Lionel's way. The creek marks the edge of his territory.

It wasn't mine. I explored it, but from the outside. I hid in the pine trees by the Catholic playing field and watched the nuns walk by, fiddling with the beads around their necks. I went into Burke's orchard and pinched apples, and several times crossed Access Road underground, through the culvert. I burrowed in the haystacks on Kelly's farm. But although I was afraid, I was only playing. My brother knew his territory in a different way. Why else would he have come back?

And unless there was in him a welling up of fear and exultation and hatred – and love, perhaps, but leave that out for the moment – how else explain the things he did? Lionel fell off a branch that bent over the creek and broke his arm on a shallow rock. He cut his foot to the bone on a broken bottle hooligans had left by the swimming hole, and ran home through the dusk leaving a trail of blood. But these are childhood happenings. I too had my share of pain and blood. I mean something else when I say fear.

The sky was full of black clouds and dark was coming early. Dad went out and cracked his strop, and Roly scuttled in. He had no idea where Lionel was. Mum said, 'That boy.' Dad said, 'I'll take the skin off his back.' But after ten minutes they began to worry. Mum stood on the back step and called, 'Ly – oh – nel.' Dad, at the back of section, barked, 'Ly-nill.' I felt their anxiety thicken into fear, but it seemed to me they were looking the wrong way. I went nervously down the path to the front steps and peered back and forth along Access Road. Two flickers of white showed in the sticky darkness, and I knew – instant recognition – that they were Lionel's bare legs as he climbed through the fence in the draught-horse paddock.

'Lynill,' I squeaked, then ran up the path to Mum: 'He's coming.'

We waited in the back yard and heard the slap of bare feet on Dad's new concrete path. Lionel burst round the corner, slid through us, eel quick, and was gone into the house. We found him curled up, sobbing, on his bed.

'What is it, Lionel? Are you hurt?' Mum cried. She sat on the bed, then lay down and put her arms around him.

'Was it Clyde?' Roly said.

Lionel kept on sobbing. Mum freed an arm and shooed us away, but we stood in the doorway, all of us fearful and needing to know.

'Lionel, darling, tell me,' she said.

He swelled, collapsed – deep inhalations, then bursts of expelled air that must, I felt, leave his body little more than dry bones in Mum's arms.

'It was – it was . . .'

'What, Lionel?'

'It was dark down there.' He began to cry, which returned him to normal and washed my fear away. Dad gave a grunt and returned to the kitchen.

'Where, Lionel? In the trees? Was someone bothering you?'

'No,' he said. 'No.'

'Did you hurt yourself?'

'No. Just dark. It was – dark.'

He spoke as if she must understand and, when she did not, fell to grizzling like a kettle. Although he made no movement, I felt him turn away from her and confine himself.

If I had been his comforter I would have known what to say. I would have said, Where was it, Lionel? In the air? In the shadows? In the water? And he would have understood.

Down-creek from the Millbrook swimming hole, after a long shallow stretch, the trees closed in, the water darkened from green to black as the bottom fell away. This was Lionel's pool for silverbellies and tommycod. Something stirred in the trees that night, something floated up from deep in the water. A cold hand touched him on the neck.

I'll have no truck with animism or forest gods but will go along with imagination peopling the dark. Lionel took a step too far. Perhaps with the aid of a movement or a sound, and with a movement in his head, the opening of a door that might have led him nowhere at another time, he created a presence – that's my amateur view. If we had been churchy, he might have glimpsed Satan. I'll leave it there – leave him grizzling on his bed, safe (or so it seemed) in Mum's arms.

Although he was nine and a hardy boy, night fears began to torment him. He heard the creaking of a wardrobe door. He heard feet whispering on the path outside his window, and something swallowing and scratching the wall, and he rose on his pillow and cried, 'Mum, Dad,' into the dark. Lionel and

Roly shared a narrow room Dad had constructed by enclosing the front porch. The built-in beds were two feet wide and the gap between them little more. When no one answered Lionel's call, he took to jumping blindly to Roly's bed, where he snuggled down beside his six-year-old brother, taking the inside place by the wall. Several times Roly tipped out on the floor. Mum and Dad gave in. They put a camp stretcher in their room – 'Only for one night, Lionel, you're not going to sleep here for ever.'

Half-waking in the small hours and hearing sounds, Lionel threw his blankets off and jumped for Roly's bed. I heard the thump from my room as he crashed into the wooden rail at the end of the double bed – heard Mum's shriek and Lionel's howl. He bruised his forehead, skinned his nose, broke a tooth. I found it the next day, an incisor, as I crawled hunting under the bed, and offered it to Lionel who, bandaged and plastered, was dozing contentedly on the living-room couch. 'Stick it up your nose,' he said.

What happened next? I don't know. That jump in the night brings memory to a close. I do know that Lionel wore a gapped smile until, as a student, he had a false tooth fitted at the Otago dental school.

EXULTATION, HATRED, I MENTIONED THEM. ABOUT THE former, I can't be precise. Shining eyes and flushed cheeks and shouts of joy that seemed to have no correlative. He came in from his outside world bursting with self – self, perhaps, is the correlative. There was a glow on him, a glow *in* him, expressed in a voice too loud, movements too violent and, it sometimes seemed, an invisible flame forking from his mouth; and it needed Mum's sharpest voice and Dad's hand slapping the table to turn these things inward, into stillness. Then Lionel would sit smouldering with his residue of joy.

It troubled Mum and pleased her in equal parts. Her puritanism rose from a natural severity of mind. She made no allowance for ease unless it filled the pause for another leap. The goal was no more than doing good – which has a disappointing sound. Lionel, stepping into her kitchen from places she would never go, troubled her as a Chinaman might have, coming through the door.

His dark moods were easier to understand. She put them down to 'growing pains'. Growth spurts, which she also watched for in Roly and me, drew off nourishment that might have gone to the brain. They enfeebled the spirits and led to moping and the sulks. Lionel, down in the dumps, was like an old dog skulking in the back of its kennel. Mum drew him out with treats and endearments, but although he might accept a biscuit or a glass of fizz, he stayed balanced on the edge of withdrawal, and she, wanting reciprocal love, could tip him back into himself with a wrong gesture or word. She tapped his shoulder in passing, and he looked sideways at the spot and shrugged off her touch as though it were a beetle. And if, caution lost, she ruffled his hair and said, 'How's my fine little man?' he shrieked with rage and ran outside, slamming the door.

We had stormy days. I locked myself in my bedroom to get away, and Lionel, crawling under the house, scratched on the floorboards: 'I'm gunna bore a hole and suck you down.' His threats mounted like spadefuls of earth. I imagined him frying me in a tin lid the way he fried silverbellies at the creek, but I never told Mum and Dad, because he whispered, 'I'll get you in the night if you pimp.' And I loved Lionel. He was bold and mysterious and he *knew*. He would fight anyone who said bad things about his sister. When he was sunny, I felt his warmth on my skin.

Although he showed no interest in music, Mum was determined he should learn. She bought an old piano with yellow keys and peeling veneer and paid for music lessons from the nuns, but it was soon clear that Lionel had no aptitude. Wooden fingers, leaden ears – poor Lionel. Soon, holding those fingers out, he showed her red weals on their backs. The teaching nun punished his mistakes with the edge of her ruler. Mum found it both cruel and unnatural. Her love of music was genuine, although she knew not the first thing about it. Liquid notes, voluminous soarings, sad fallings-away – those were her music, in which she found, by some alchemy or transmutation, lessons in love and endeavour and sacrifice. That those women in black, women with wasted lives (her words), should damage perfection with a ruler's edge, filled her with outrage and disgust, and she went to the school and told the head nun so. Lionel's musical education came to an end. And Mum's grievance against the nuns grew into an obsession. So I blame her . . .

At five o'clock in the winter dusk, in his tenth year, Lionel crept through the macrocarpa hedge, through the wattle grove and past the two gravel courts where the Holy Cross Tennis Club played its weekend matches, and came to the school. The caretaker stored his tools in a cupboard at the back of the shelter shed. Lionel took a spade and smashed the window glass in the lower classroom. He put his arm through the hole and unlatched the window, then fetched a box from the cupboard and used it as a stool to climb inside. It took courage in the thickening dusk and creaking silence. I hear him gulping, whimpering perhaps, as he parts shadows and edges them away. He empties the drawers in the teacher's table, makes a pile of dusters and chalk boxes and books, and pours a bottle of ink over it. He slinks about the room, tipping inkwells on desks. Some he splashes on the books inside. He strips down maps and charts and posters from the walls – Jesus with a bleeding heart? – and tears them into pieces. Lionel is a cat; he has teeth and claws and yellow eyes. A pity that, at the end, he turns into a dog – peeing on the teacher's chair.

Constable Norton was a Catholic. He found the culprit with God's help. A big man, red faced and meaty handed, he entered our house by the front door.

'So this is the young scallywag.'

Mum took Roly and me into the kitchen, so I don't know what else he said.

'Will they put him in prison?'

'Kids don't go,' Roly said.

'Shush.' Mum was listening at the door.

'They'll give him the cat and nine tails,' Roly said.

I started to cry.

'Shush,' Mum hissed. She was ready to rush into the sitting room and fight the Catholics to save her son.

But Constable Norton didn't flog Lionel or give him more than a telling off. Dad flogged him instead, when the constable was gone.

I'm getting carried away – tears in my eyes – so let me change that. Dad gave him a whipping. Instead of a willow stick he used his leather belt from the wardrobe. Mum took Roly and me up past the dunny into the garden so we wouldn't hear the hits and hear Lionel howl. She made us put our fingers in our ears. She bit her lips until they bled. I believe that sentence when I read it in books. Mum wiped blood from her mouth.

I don't know how much Dad payed to fix the damage – two or three weeks' wages perhaps. Lionel had a day off school with iodine on his legs.

When Roly and I got home, Mum took all three of us up to the back of the section.

'From now on this is the boundary. You never go through the hedge, any of you. Do you promise?'

'Yes, Mum,' we said.

'And if you ever see any nuns . . .' She did not finish.

That night Lionel, prompted by Mum, sidled up to Dad's

shoulder as he sat by the kitchen stove.

'Dad, I just want to say I'm sorry.'

Dad patted him. 'It's all right, son. It's all forgotten.'

I know Lionel's expressions. He would not forget.

A perfect end to this story would be that Lionel became a Catholic when he grew up, but he did not. Nor did Roly, nor did I.

four

SUMMER RAIN BRUSHES OUR SUBURB, LEAVING DICKIE'S
roses bedewed. He dips his face in the petals, then wipes his
wet cheeks with a handkerchief. Dickie is hunting for a perfect
bloom, which he'll snip with his secateurs and carry inside to
me. There'll be no tumble of words: roses silence him. He'll
simply hold it out, a gift needing no explanation, and as long as
I can keep myself confined in the marriage suite of our present
days I'll take my pleasure of the perfect thing, its tenderness
and colour – always red – and the grasp its central petals keep
on the secret within. I'll fetch a vase and place Dickie's rose on

the mantelpiece, and all through the day, coming and going, I'll accept his gift – and yet, after each flush of pleasure, I'll find uncurling in my brain that dreadful poem:

> O Rose thou art sick!
> The invisible worm
> That flies in the night
> In the howling storm
> Has found out thy bed
> Of crimson joy . . .

I really can't put down the last two lines. 'Dreadful' is not a word I choose lightly. I'm overflowing with dread.

But Dickie is outside that purview. Look at him now, breathless and intent – *scarred* and breathless and intent – confined within a moment that fills him to his fingertips and stretches as wide as the world.

He's in the fours semi-final at his bowling club. The greens will dry out in the sun and he'll head off in his whites as soon as he has watched me envase my rose. It's not a big tournament, just 'something to keep us old fellers amused'. Dickie plays lead. He likes that better than skip. He can lay a perfect platform and 'if the buggers foul it up that's their look-out'. How quotable he is, even when he says nothing original. Unlike my mother, I never wanted a man with thoughts in his head.

❖ ❖ ❖

I WENT OUT IN THE AFTERNOON TO DO MY BIT OF shopping: milk, tomatoes, hummus and four slices of ham off the bone (three for Dickie, one for me). We'll eat a cold dinner and drink a bottle of pinot gris. On my way home, lugging my green bag to save the world from plastic, I slipped through the bowling club gate and sat on a bench to watch my husband at play. He polishes his bowl with a yellow cloth, as careful with it as with his roses, and sends it on its syrupy roll along the grass. I love the way those heavy balls slow down but keep turning over, like thoughts before sleep; how they seem mistaken, wide of the mark (that chaste little kitty, not caring who takes her in the end), and then haul themselves in as though the magnetic and geographical poles change places and find, impossibly, a dozen degrees of angle and two more turns, and kiss, or is it rub, their object of desire, which shifts a centimetre or two while keeping secure that caress on her cheek. Dickie can make it happen. I saw him work the magic with his first bowl and felt my blood quicken along with his. It did not matter that the opposing lead knocked his bowl away, or that his second plopped into the ditch. Dickie had had his moment and increased himself. Perhaps he had added some extra minutes to his life – or subtracted them. No matter which. The moment was the thing and I carried my share of it away, my green bag lighter.

Lightness is an old friend, almost forgotten. The first time I danced with Dickie I was lifted up. In spite of my quickness, I'm not a good dancer. It's a matter of rhythm. Nothing moves in me, so I feel as if my feet are plugging through sticky mud like that between the mangroves and the tide-line where Loomis Creek meets the sea at the head of the harbour.

It was a muddy dance in the RSA hall. Insinuating oily boys, emboldened by the beer they went out to their cars to drink, rolled their knobby loins over my tummy at every turn. Loud insinuation, if that's possible; back-and-forth commentary between the clown you were dancing with and his Brylcreemed cobbers at the door. I'm being unfair, but that's the measure of my discontent. I was not seeking anything impossible, just more than 'leg over', something more than 'turning it up'. I was looking for love – and who is not? – and wanting a boy who did not wear toughness like a rubbery skin; who might shed his false persona at a word I would find, and offer in return some word of his own.

It makes me smile. I look up from my writing and see myself in the window pane, bending my lips. It's not in derision or with superior knowledge. I have learned nothing and I'm lost. My smile at myself says, Come back to me, I never meant to let you go.

I'd had enough of those Loomis boys. If I work at it now I can tell them apart and even gather half a dozen names, but mostly they arrange themselves in my mind like nine-pins and I clatter them into oblivion. I went to the cloakroom for my coat. A wintry wind blew outside and I had a long trudge up the hill. The Beaches were no longer in Access Road but had shifted to a grander house in Te Atatu Road, with views across the harbour to the Chelsea Sugar Works and Rangitoto frowning beyond. Going home alone from the dance didn't bother me. I felt upright and pale and pure as I emerged from the cloakroom in my belted coat. I tied a scarf over my hair.

'Hey, don't put out the light,' Dickie Pinker said.

I knew that boy emerging from the midwinter dark. I saw that at twenty-one – quick arithmetic – he had shed the ugly certainties I had observed across the divide separating a second-year nobody from the First Fifteen rugby star. Our school was Avondale College; I travelled there from Te Atatu Corner on the bus. Dickie Pinker vanished from it at the end of that year, and I heard no more of him until his name and photograph showed up in the *Herald* sporting pages: scoring machine, future All Black. So the gap was still there, widened now by my revised requirements in a man

I was nineteen. I was a virgin. No one was having me cheaply. More than smart words were needed to untie the strings that held me tight. More than a cheeky grin, more than photographs in the *Herald*. Yet when Dickie Pinker smiled at me from the hall doorway, my heart turned over. You find that phrase in romantic novels, although I'm not sure Georgette uses it. The words sound right and physiologically there's a lurch. The blood races. On that Saturday night my face turned scarlet, which I like to avoid with my red hair.

I went back to the cloakroom, took off my head scarf and coat, and cooled my cheeks at the basin. I fluffed up my hair and patted it down. I danced with Dickie Pinker, moving with lightness and grace. And Dickie? He was blunted. We were equals in affecting each other.

He had come to our Loomis dance from Avondale with one of his Suburbs Rugby Football Club mates. Stardom had lifted him above club rivalries, and he was in no danger in Loomis. There was a ring of influence around him, which he was aware of and confused a little by. He behaved with assurance on a ground of uncertainty. His simplicity, his glamour were two sides of a coin. I was not immune to the heads side, but the other (can't call it 'tails'), with confusion caught in it like a fish in a net, attracted me more. Although I knew he could have what he wanted, including me, my feeling for him as we danced was protective.

'I remember you from school,' I said.

'Yeah? I remember you.'

'Liar.'

I won't carry on with our inanities, although they're cemented in my mind. I don't really need to put Dickie and Rowan in review. Ask for any primal event, ask for any landmark, I'll unroll the scroll, I'll parrot the exchanges. I'm more concerned with what other people were doing, and there I'm mostly in the dark. What was Lionel doing that night (he was at the dance), and what was Clyde Buckley doing?

CLYDE BUCKLEY. THERE'S A NAME. THERE'S A FACE AND a set of behaviours. I can't remember my first sight of him:

Clyde was always there, throwing Lionel's sheath knife at a cardboard box with Tojo drawn in crayons on the side, reading comics with him on the front steps, eating stolen apples in the scrub next door. The list goes on. Yet Clyde was not an Access Road boy; he came from a railway house on the far side of the creek, where the road climbed towards the jam factory and Loomis town. His father was a linesman, his mother a hump-shouldered woman with ankles always bandaged because of a skin disease. There were three older brothers and a sister, all gone and, as far as I could tell, forgotten.

Clyde fastened himself on Lionel as an out-of-school friend. At school he was solitary, while Lionel ran with the gang that ruled the playground. But every afternoon, soon after three o'clock, Clyde Buckley was somewhere about our section, with Lionel gravitating towards him. By some reversal, perhaps by no more than a pressure of will, outside school, even in places Lionel had made for himself – his hidey-hole under the house, behind the chimney base, his mudslide on the bank by the culvert – Clyde was the one who made the moves. When I see them running, it's Clyde in the lead, not because he's faster but because he knows the way. He hasn't yet told Lionel what it is. Lionel follows because he needs to know.

Clyde was a large-bodied boy, thick rather than fat. He was short in his limbs, as though they had stopped growing while his body kept on, but large in his face, where his skin was at the full stretch of its elasticity. He kept himself side-on when talking, and spoke no more than he needed to, and then not well, with a thickened tongue. His eyes shone as though coated with oil, but seemed not to see, unless it was something going on in his head.

I kept away from Clyde, giving his bad smell as my reason.

'Yeah,' Lionel said, 'they've got their bath filled up with coal.'

I'm not going to waste time on Clyde Buckley. I've got better memories. When we shifted to Te Atatu Road he was gone from our lives. I passed him now and then in town, but he turned his head away, which was fine. I had no wish to say hello. Now and then he showed up at the town-hall pictures or a dance, but he had never approached me until the night I met Dickie Pinker.

Dickie kept at my side between dances. We had slipped together into an enclosure of ease, warmer than the surrounding air, where every word we spoke – simple, silly words – had the sound of truth. I found my partner the way pieces of a jigsaw puzzle fit together: this goes with that, the picture builds. We danced a foxtrot, then a waltz, and were sitting out the third dance when Clyde Buckley came from somewhere unseen and stood at my side, with his heavy lower leg touching my calf.

'Can I have this dance?' he said in his thick-tongued voice.

I was dismayed. I did not want Dickie Pinker thinking that this ugly sweat-smelling boy – I'll change that 'boy'; Clyde was a man of twenty-two or thereabouts – had a connection with me or any knowledge of who I was.

Without looking at him I shook my head.

'Rowan?' he said.

Dickie Pinker leaned forward. His forearm on the back of my chair fell warm against my neck.

'Shove off, buddy. She said no.'

Most boys would have said 'mate'. I thought 'buddy' marvellous. It lifted me out of Loomis into the world of romance. Clyde turned and plodded through the couples moving on to the floor. With a sideways glance and a little sigh of relief, I saw him go out of the hall – and here is a strange thing: I never saw Clyde Buckley again. I've had no glimpse of him since that night almost sixty years ago. Mind you, I was not in Loomis very much. My life opened out; I freed my limbs. Together Dickie and I untied the knots that bound me – knots of misinformed expectation, of romantic illusion, of snobbery and puritanism and many more – and Dickie, soon enough (although not that night), was able to crack the best joke of his life: 'Rowan my boat'.

BUT I CAN'T LEAVE CLYDE BUCKLEY YET, IF I'M TO BE honest. He lived over the creek from us by the jam factory for most of my girlhood, and has marked me with memories like welts on my skin. They don't bother me, they don't itch, but now and then I notice them and they wriggle like worms. Yet I'm innocent, I swear.

How old was I? Eight? Nine? It's a movie show without

credits, and a black screen at the start and end. Pine trees. There's no hush like pine hush. I'm at the little creek running through the grove by the Catholic playing field. Although it is Sunday, no nuns walk on the path. My game is to cover the water with a pine-needle mat. Roly is with me. He builds a needle mountain and tries to crawl inside. That's scene one. Now here comes Clyde Buckley: scene two. He carries a bird's nest like a salad bowl and shows us six naked baby birds inside. They seem to be sleeping, although one opens its beak in a half-hearted way. I stroke their heads with my fingertip. They stir but don't open their spoon-shaped eyes.

'What are you going to do with them?' Roly asks.

'Show you,' Clyde says.

I'll be quick. He found a stick and fitted it over the creek at its narrowest part, little more than a metre. He took a reel of cotton (black cotton) from his pocket – Clyde was prepared – and hung the baby birds on the stick by their necks. They dangled over the water like naked murderers. Clyde took half a razor blade from his shirt pocket and went along the row cutting off heads. One by one the bodies plopped into the water.

There, that's done. As usual, I want to be sick.

There's a scene that shows me running home. Only me. In real life Roly ran after me, yelling, 'Rowan, wait.' Did I, did he, tell Mum? Did she go after Clyde? I don't know. There's nothing at the start or the end. A thing I can't hide from, though, is that I watched until the last cut was made and the last body sank through my pine-needle mat. So how can I say I'm innocent?

How I long for Dickie to come home.

❀ ❀ ❀

I GREW UP WITHOUT AN IDEA OF SIN BUT WITH 'NAUGHTY' emplaced in my mind. What a kind word by comparison, and kind, too, the smack on the back of the hand that went with it. These days I drift in the shoal of 'cruelty' and 'iniquity'. I gasp for air and grasp at innocence. But what is that? I'm over-brimming now with the self I chose to be.

Let me move aside from that imagery and be quick.

It is the year of the baby birds and perhaps a year before Lionel's raid on the Catholic school. He leads me by the hand, which I don't like. I shake myself free. We're in Kelly's farm, among the haystacks. My legs prickle with heat rash and I want to go home, but Lionel has promised me sixpence if I come as far as Burke's orchard. There, in the bottom corner, Clyde Buckley waits.

'OK, once,' Lionel says.

'All right,' Clyde Buckley says in his thick voice.

Lionel turns to me. 'Go on,' he orders.

It had seemed a small thing, but the fog of difference enclosing Clyde made it large – so I said no, and backed away and turned to run.

Lionel grabbed my arm.

[61]

'No quitting,' he said. 'Come on, it's easy. Just do it quick. You don't have to pull them down all the way.' He held me facing Clyde, and lifted the front of my dress. 'Else no sixpence.'

Sixpence meant things beyond my reach – a custard pie, a big ice cream, bags of sherbet – so I turned my head away from Clyde, made myself absent, hooked my finger in my pants and pulled the leg across, letting Clyde see. He had time to bend down and breathe – I felt his wet breath on me – then I let the elastic go and jerked my dress free from Lionel's hand.

'That's not a real look,' Clyde said.

'Too bad. It's all,' Lionel said.

'Hey –' But he was blunted by what he had seen.

I turned and ran, with Lionel yelling after me: 'You better not tell, Rowan.'

'Sixpence then,' I cried back – and didn't tell, have told no one to this day – and he paid me. It doesn't seem a dreadful sin. Clyde Buckley is dreadful, and Lionel too, in a more sophisticated way, but not me. The girl part of me I'd let Clyde see was just a part, although it was dirty in two ways. I didn't know more than a whisper about the second, and wasn't curious; but it was what Clyde Buckley was after, I knew that. So I felt sick, and eager for my sixpence to make me better. I didn't blame Lionel. All he was after was the money, and that was all right. He got, he boasted to me in a whisper, half a crown, which Clyde had stolen from his mother's purse – Clyde boasting too, to make himself victor.

That's number two of my short films of innocence, which

yet raises a welt on my mind. Why the confusion? I can only say, Because my life cannot be broken into bits and viewed that way. Yet I must try.

So here's a third. I don't play an active part in it, but it answered my need to know and it played a part in me. I wish the agent had been different.

Let me see: I creep in the culvert. The water barely trickles, so it's summer. I'm able to keep my feet dry. My carefulness, my creeping, mean I'm a spy. My age? Eleven? My knowledge is that Lionel has moved somewhere I can't go, and what he finds makes him feral, coarse, hungry and satisfied. All I am is hot.

I watch him framed in the culvert mouth. He's a round picture on a wall. A flash like electricity outlines him as he steps into the sun. He turns side-on and I close my eyes to be invisible if he looks back. When I open them, Lionel is gone. I start to hurry, careless of the sludge. If I lose him I am blood-less and locked for ever in this cave.

The swamp runs widening for fifty yards. I follow Lionel's oozing steps until I come to willow trees and water. Voices there. Lionel's voice. Clyde Buckley's voice. I make no sense of what they're saying and, from my hiding place, very little sense of what I see. Those things poking from their unbut-toned flies are penises, I'm sure of that. I've glimpsed, I've even seen Lionel's and Roly's many times, just as now and then, by accident, they've seen me. These parts of us must be covered, although they're nothing to get upset about. But these huge things Lionel and Clyde hold, are they penises? They look as big as my arm. And when they stop stroking and rubbing and put them together like crossed swords to see whose is bigger – it's Clyde's, by a long way – I find myself choking with a kind of grief. It's not true, what I've been told. I had pictured penises growing as long as butter beans and no fatter, but these, especially Clyde's, are huge and thick and blunt and cruel, and have fat red bits on the end.

Now and then I've tried to find an adjective for erect penises – not that I've seen many: three in fact, Lionel's and Clyde's on that day, and Dickie's of course. Three. Believe it or not. But I've seen the thing in books and tried for a word – and now I have it. Overweening. If I fit it into that episode in the willow trees, it satisfies my need for control of what I see.

I won't stay now for the rest of it, although I stayed then – the renewed rubbing and what Clyde called the shooting off – but creep away and slop through the culvert again, then stand up straight and run through Kelly's paddocks and burst into the kitchen and into the bathroom, where I wash my hands as though they have been the busy ones, and wash my face as though it's my mind.

There's nothing to be excited about. It became a small thing as I grew older. I suppose I can say I was innocent. It will do. But 'overweening' – that's the word. How clever of me to find it.

five

HERE IS A STRANGE THING ABOUT MY BROTHERS: LIONEL
has an outline and Roly is smudged. I can be kinder to my
younger brother than that: Roly stands in the dappled shade.

Because Avondale College didn't open until 1945, Lionel
went to Mt Albert Grammar. His schooling gets away from
me. Roly joined me at Avondale where I passed everything
with high marks. Roly failed. He was in a technical form, doing woodwork and metalwork. As a practical boy he should
have done well, but school and Roly never fitted. The air was
unbreathable in a classroom. He forgot what his hands should

do. He forgot language. Because he joked and smiled and woke up with a start, his classmates liked him. So did several of the teachers. Others caned him. Roly did not seem to care. It was as if caning stood in the natural order of things.

There was nothing wrong with my brother. There were, there are, more things right than the world with its systems will accommodate. One teacher rapped him on the head with his knuckles: 'Born without a brain, eh, Beach? Solid bone in there.' Oh no, Mr Teacher, more things than you could ever know. He had his dreaming; he had his making – dreaming of real things, not phantoms or fulfilments; making things in his mind and then joining mind with hands and building a pine-needle mountain to wriggle inside.

I have to admit there was no long-term purpose. Roly did not see beyond his fingertips or feel out tomorrow with his mind. But he knew from the moment he could run a wobbly furrow through the soil with his finger and sprinkle radish seeds in it that plants require their whole season to grow.

Our mother made no bones about her disappointment in Roly. Dad loved him best. In memory, his hand rests on Roly's shoulder, his fist, loosely curled, bangs him on top of his head. They talk to each other in monosyllables. In the garden Dad points and Roly brings him what he needs – a bucketful of compost, his knife to cut the seed potatoes. The sun comes out from behind a cloud. Roly digs the handkerchief out of Dad's pocket and knots the corners and hands it to him, and Dad stops digging to fit it on his head.

On Saturdays Roly sits on the bar of Dad's bike and they ride off to watch the football on Loomis domain. They go eel fishing in the creek. And Dad spends hours with Roly building a canoe from corrugated iron; then they build a better one when Roly sinks the first in the rapids below the swing bridge. So, love, uncomplicated, flowing two ways – I'm tempted to write like honey, and yes, I will – it flowed like honey.

Mum's love was of a different sort. She spent hours helping Roly with his schoolwork. Sitting at the kitchen table, with her finger directing his pencil, and sometimes with her arm around him, she became convinced he understood. Long division: he could do it. Spelling: he could remember that 'i' came before 'e' except after 'c'. She helped him with the technical drawing that was part of his woodwork course. But he could never be quick enough for her. She felt a kind of shame in having a child who was 'slow', and in the end she jumped from her chair and flung herself away. 'You're not trying, Roland. I don't know how I came to have such a stupid boy.' Then Roly sat at the table, grinning to himself. I think he grinned to stop himself from crying.

Lionel protected him the way he protected me. It was a form of self-expression. He also released his cruelty on him. 'A pinch and a punch for the first of the month,' he said on every first of the month. His projecting middle knuckle raised an egg-sized lump on Roly's forearm. (He did the same, more softly, to me, but I punched back: 'A pinch and a punch for the first of the month, and no returns. You forgot that.' I dug my fingernails into my pinch and my middle knuckle into his breastbone.)

Roly cried when Lionel hurt him, although he never cried at school. He was an easy laugher too. He laughed every time Lionel said cow juice instead of milk and cackle-berries instead of eggs. When Roly started using Lionel's jokes, Lionel stopped. His dumb small brother devalued them. 'Yum, yum pig's bum makes good chewing gum.' He said it no more. He stopped his raucous chant: 'Once aboard the lugger and the girl is mine.' Then Roly, with no one to copy, fell silent too.

Silence is what I remember best about him. He chattered as a small boy; he mimicked and joked and interjected when he was older; but in his teens he rarely opened his mouth. Looking at his years, I see that his wrapping up of himself came with puberty. I've mentioned Lionel's in its most obvious (overweening) manifestation, but Roly gave no evidence of that sort. There was body hair and secrecy and silence and the deepening of his voice, but perhaps its plainest expression was his stepping away from Lionel. He was shorter than his older brother but more muscular. If Lionel came at him with a physical threat, Roly would simply hold him and push him away. With me he became more distant and courteous. He gave our difference its due. It was not entirely something he had learned from Mum, but came equally from the intertwined ways we had travelled and his apprehension of their untangling now. I caught him looking at me as though working me out, and felt like a page in a book with Roly's finger moving along the lines. He wondered who I was. He acknowledged the strangeness of a sister.

Roly turned fifteen, and although Mum disagreed, and fought her case, Dad insisted there was no point in his staying at school. His love for Roly gave him the strength to over-rule her. He would find Roly a job in the shoemaking factory. Oh no, never! Mum would blockade the station before letting Roly climb on that morning train. They finally agreed on a bricklaying apprenticeship. But Roly, it turned out, had no feeling for bricks: too slow with his hands, too imprecise with his eye. He took labouring jobs in vineyards and worked the picking season in orchards. For a while he was at the freezing works at Westfield – which meant climbing on two trains – and later at the city markets, humping fruit and vegetables around. He claimed to like it, and looked blankly at me when I said, 'Lifting, carrying, putting down'; and even more blankly when, repairing my nastiness, 'It gives you time to think about things.'

Then, at eighteen, Roly upsticks (Lionel's word for the event) and was gone. We were in our Te Atatu Road house by that time, a move beyond Mum and Dad's expectations, made possible by a legacy on Mum's father's death. She had thought herself written out of his will, but no, there it was, her one-third – enough for a better house, and enough to educate her children. Now, Roland, I hear her inward cry, now you can have a second chance.

He withstood her pressure for a year and then he bolted.

I had more than a feeling it would happen. I had evidence: his rucksack planted behind a hydrangea bush by the gate. I opened it, of course: a work shirt, work trousers (he left his best clothes behind, which I found significant), underclothes, socks, sandshoes (which, in fact, were his best shoes), a tin plate (brand new), and a knife, fork and spoon taken from our cutlery drawer. There was also a Zane Grey novel with a page turned down (it took him a month to finish a book, even a Western).

It wasn't late, but his bedroom light was off. I knocked softly on the door and went in.

'You forgot your toothbrush and you should take some handkerchiefs.'

He rose from the pillow. Light from a street lamp yellowed one side of his face.

'Don't tell, Rowan.'

'I won't. Where are you going?'

'I'll hitch-hike for a while. Then I'll get a job on an orchard.'

'Where?'

'I dunno. Where I find one, I guess.'

The gilded half of his face was smiling quietly. I thought, He's only got half a brain.

'How about money?'

'I've saved up.'

'Will you write to them?'

'I was going to put a note in the letterbox, but you can tell them now, eh? Not till tomorrow night.'

'Not on your life. Mum'll kill me.'

'OK.' He never argued.

'Are you coming back ever?'

'Sometimes, I guess.'

'Come at Christmas, Roly. For Dad.'

'OK, I suppose.'

I felt I was picking things off the top of his mind and not reaching deeper inside.

'Write to them a bit. Just a note will do.'

'OK,' again.

I longed to give advice but couldn't find any, so I kissed him on the forehead and went to my room. Waking in the morning, I heard him in the kitchen, moving in his usual way – quiet with his Weetbix, quiet with his cup of tea – and heard the murmur of Mum's voice as she came from her bedroom to see him off. I knelt at my window and watched my brother go. I pinched the curtains under my chin, framing my face, with the half-romantic notion of giving Roly an image to remember; but he pulled his rucksack from the hydrangea bush, closed the gate quietly and walked away without looking back; and I knew that for him leaving home was no big thing, it was his next step.

When she found his note, Mum had no one to burst her storm on. She was in her still and dangerous state when I arrived home.

'Did you know about Roland?'

'No. What's happened?' I said.

'Read that.'

Dear Mum and Dad, he wrote, I'm heading down south to look for a job. I'll write at Christmas. Love, Roly. P.S. Thanks for everything.

'Christmas,' Mum said. 'We've just had Christmas. He'll write in a year. And what a lovely afterthought. Thanks for everything. If he only knew . . .'

'He'll be all right, Mum. He's eighteen.'

'You knew. I bet you knew.'

'No, no,' I lied.

Mum sat down at the table and gave a big farewell sob. She covered her face. I made a cup of tea.

'I phoned Constable Norton – the fat fool,' she said.

'Mum, they can't—'

'I know they can't. He asked how old Roland was and when I said eighteen . . . What can Roland do? He's got no skills. What sort of job can he find?'

'Picking fruit.'

'Picking fruit,' Mum spat. 'After eighteen years of trying with him – picking fruit.' She plucked a banana from the bowl and threw it backhanded across the room, where it bounced off the wall and sat grinning on a chair.

'Not bananas, we don't grow those,' I said.

'You knew. The pair of you. Thank God for Lionel.'

When Dad came home and read the note he sighed and sat down in the chair Mum had left pushed out at the table.

'So,' he said.

'Is that all you can say?'

'Well, Isobel, he's eighteen –'

'What's so magical about that age?'

'– and he's old enough to make his own decisions.'

'See what he says. See it.' She nailed the note to the table with her finger. '"Thanks for everything." Isn't that nice?'

But Dad read the postscript differently. He saw that Roly meant 'every thing' – their love and care and attention – every thing in his ordinary and magical eighteen years. The post-script was the best gift Dad ever had. Lionel found Roly's note in his wallet when the police handed it to him after Dad died.

YOU PLUNGE DOWN INTO LOOMIS FROM TE ATATU Corner, past the square-shouldered school and across the bridge, where new shops began to line the Great North Road shortly before the Beaches moved from Access Road. I went that way no longer, unless to the pictures or a dance. Te Atatu Corner had shops of its own and a bus stop pointing the way I wanted to go: into the city and a life as free as the one Roly set off to find. The bus put me down in Karangahape Road, where I climbed on the Mt Eden tram. A ten-minute ride, then I descended, ladylike, into the teeming street between rows of shops later designated a 'village'. I walked to the training ground for my future life, the Teachers' College, and found friendship and contentment there.

Mine is a nature requiring only a modest inflow of happiness. I don't need it in large gulps; and I can endure times of drought as long as they don't go on too long. (I think perhaps I'm describing everyone.) The Teachers' College laid down a water table in me that has lasted my whole life, with ups and downs – but this metaphor is cracking under the strain. Just let me say I had three happy years at Mt Eden – and outside the college, in my second year, I became the official girlfriend of a rugby star.

I found, too, another source of happiness. There was another fresh-flowing stream in me. (There I go again.) In my third year the College approved of my taking Stage One English at the university, and how I drank those studies down. The books, the books! The poetry, the novels, the plays! I'll get away from liquids and say I ate a three-course meal. I also began writing poetry (although in honesty it was merely verse – except for a line or two, a line or two). Mum loved it. She clutched it to her heart, literally: held one of my efforts, crumpled, smudged with flour, against her apron, and cried, 'That last line is beautiful.' Dad said, 'Very nice, Rowan.' And it *was* nice, it was pretty in a watercoloury way – sky with clouds, stream with reflections. I walked along the other side of a wall from poetry, I see that now; but with other people's – Yeats's, Keats's, John Donne's (my tastes were as various as that) – I jumped the wall; I bounced over like a spring lamb and then walked, serious but fizzing inside, among the words, among the rhymes, tasting and swallowing the beauty and the pain.

I drank novels in long draughts and wanted to retire permanently from my world into theirs.

Reading shut Dickie Pinker out of my head for days on end. It gave me a sense of my largeness – look, I can go there, and there, and spread myself out, so many rooms, so many landscapes, so many worlds with people in them – and produced in me twitches of alarm about Dickie. How large he was in so many ways – overweening – but in others how small.

Yet my chief happiness lay in Dickie Pinker. Part of it came from liking him so much – his good humour, his generosity, his surprising gentleness – and part from being attached to him in his career. Dickie owned a Ford Prefect car. He called for me each Saturday, came inside to say hello to Mum and shake Dad's hand, then we drove to wherever his Suburbs team was playing – Otahuhu, Takapuna, sometimes Eden Park. I watched him sidestep and sell dummies, and as I learned about rugby, came to understand how good he was. I loved the adulation people poured on him and took little sips of it myself when I saw their eyes light on me, the girlfriend. It's a funny brew; has the taste of nectar but leaves you bad-tempered when the flow runs out – I think even Dickie felt that. The first year I was with him, he was selected for the Auckland team and I had to step back – no room for girlfriends at the higher level. He played in the Junior All Blacks too, and next year, everybody said, it would be the All Blacks, who were short of a good first five-eighths.

He had no summer sport, no cricket, no tennis, and nor did

I, so we went to the beach, where he tanned himself almost black, while I tried for a lemonade glow on my pale skin. If I'm to be truthful, our main sport in that long summer was sex. He was a bit slam bang at the beginning, but his instinct was for gentleness and that's my preference too, in spite of the sensualist residing in me – my mother's daughter. So we learned to be very good with each other, Dickie and me, me and Dickie, and passed the summer in a subdued blaze of contentment. My worry was getting pregnant, even though, after several tries, I'd found a doctor willing to fit me with a diaphragm. Those things could fail. And Dickie, for all his shortish stature, was exceptionally (I had his word for it) long and thick down there, and once or twice dislodged the wretched thing. I made him wear rubbers after that.

Why am I putting this down? Because that summer was so large and long. It floats in my being like a time capsule, bouncing where it touches and making me sing. Even the worry, the devices, make me sing. I think of that summer as our honeymoon.

A dark moon rose over us when the season changed. Such a complicated mechanism, the knee. There's a thing deep inside called the cruciate ligament. Playing against Ponsonby, Dickie was tackled from two sides, a hulking forward at his shoulders, a skinny winger hugging his boots, and his knee bent sideways like a rhubarb stalk, almost to the point of snapping. I heard him scream – such a girlish cry. The ligament snapped like frayed string. Then Dickie sat howling silently, and throwing back his head until it seemed his neck ligaments would break too. His season was over. And Dickie was over, the Dickie I knew. He never came back, the footballer or the rowdy, gentle boy.

In the weeks that followed, watching him hobble on sticks, watching him bite the rotten world with his unspoiled teeth, finding him several times weeping silently, I knew that I must marry him soon.

I did that. I married the snarling bugger. Excuse my language. It's the best way of describing him, the sad, snarling bugger I loved. We set up house in half a house in Avondale and I went on with my probationary teaching year while he worked in his father's hardware shop. I must be fair to him. His great feast on oysters and pudding was snatched away; and he had even more to endure – pity, which he could not stand, and, amazingly, the contempt of those who looked on the tearing of a ligament as a deficiency in character. Dickie blinked at them and didn't know what to say. I got rid of them: 'Get out of my house and don't come back.' I felt like saying it to Dickie too at times.

So we went on – and, feeling anger simmer again, I'll stop. There were good years, bad years, years that mixed the two, and here we are. Choosing how to call the time we're enjoying now is like the shell game.

THE LAST TIME I VISITED MY DENTIST HE SPENT MORE time at the computer than looking in my mouth. One of my molars had lost a filling (black amalgam, put in when I was a girl) and was, in his words, no longer viable. He would reduce it to a stump and fit a brand-new homemade tooth on top. He looked at me anxiously when he told me the price. Go ahead, I said. He did some drilling, absolutely painless, then entered this and that on the computer, a process that probably requires great skill, while I chatted with his nurse (a pleasant girl wearing braces that I hope she got a discount on). The computer drew up plans for my new tooth, then a machine in the corner, grating unpleasantly, fashioned it from a block of white stuff whose name I forget. Michelangelo should have had one of those. The dentist fixed my molar on the stump with magic glue. All done. I paid on the spot.

Lionel was too early for one of those machines. People who went to him told me he was a good dentist – friendly, patient, soft with his hands, and apologetic on the rare occasions he needed to be. It made me wonder. Friendliness and patience did not come easily to Lionel. Mum had to prompt him to apologise. (Like the time Dad whipped him, after the Catholic school.) Do they teach professional manners at the dental school? For my kind and cruel brother the lesson must have been hard.

There was money from Mum's legacy to help him through the course. But why a dentist? He was wild, free roaming, undisciplined. How could he choose the confines of the human mouth? Clean fingers and sterilised probes, nit-picking drills – that wasn't Lionel. I asked him once, carelessly, and he turned white with rage. 'I'd love to get you in my fucking chair,' he said.

Dentistry is an honourable trade. It's useful and highly skilled and isn't the technology wonderful? I can imagine youngsters choosing it out of interest. So why do I imagine that Lionel was punishing himself?

He stayed at school until he was eighteen but wasn't smart enough for medicine, which Mum wanted for him desperately. Law would have been all right, although she didn't fully trust 'those men in wigs', and neither did Dad. Lionel said they were 'a bunch of bloody sharks'; and I told him if that was the case he would fit in nicely, meaning it, in a back-handed way, as a compliment. He understood and bared his teeth at me: 'I know where I'm going.' Mum sighed and accepted it. A dentist was a professional after all. Lionel lifted the Beaches out of the bootmaker class.

He came to dinner with Dickie and me after his course was over and before heading south for his first job. I was still teaching, and Dickie, no longer savage about his lost 'big chance', was simply down in the dumps, where he was to slop around for a few years yet.

My brother and my husband, or, to place them in their order of importance, my husband and my brother, had met only half a dozen times. Their dislike of each other was instinctive. Dickie had been king of the sidestep on the field but Lionel's mental sidestep left him grasping at air. Lionel had the quicker mind and a hungry reading of weakness, while Dickie had his weakness laid out for all to see. But Dickie was immoveable in his centre. A block of stone stood there with *Pinker* engraved on the side. And I was beginning to detect a resonance, a humming in the air, as if someone (it had to be Dickie himself) had struck it with a mallet and made it sing. With hindsight, I'll supply the words: I might have missed out on what I wanted, but by God I'm going to make a killing at something else. It was faint at that time, as I said, and several twisting corridors of self-pity had to be laboured through yet.

Lionel isolated the self-pity. He fed commiseration into it. He made Dickie walk across the room and back, and do it again, to see how he limped.

'My God, that's bad. You poor bugger. Is that the leg you did your sidestep off?'

'I could step off both feet,' Dickie boasted.

'But your knee just collapses now? Will you always limp?'

'There's an operation for it but I can't play again.'

'Poor bugger. No All Blacks, eh? Does it hurt?'

'Aches a bit,' Dickie said. He was growing suspicious.

'I meant playing for New Zealand, losing a chance like that. I reckon I'd sit down and cry.'

Dickie said nothing.

'It'd break your heart,' Lionel went on.

'Break your fucking jaw,' I heard Dickie mutter, and I said,

'I'm sorry there's no pudding. But I've got some of Mum's chocolate sponge.'

'God save me from Mum's cooking,' Lionel said. 'Can we have some coffee?'

The coffee age, just arriving, had not arrived at our house. I made tea and came back in time to hear Lionel say, '– spend your life behind a counter.'

'It's better than swabbing out people's mouths,' Dickie said.

Lionel kept his temper. 'There's more to it than that. And more money than selling nails and tacks.'

'You reckon?' Dickie said, and I caught the sound of mallet on stone.

'Hey, though, you don't have to give up playing sport. You could be an All Black at bowls. Or how about croquet?'

'What's *your* sport? Pulling your pud?' Dickie said.

Sometimes Lionel went white with anger and sometimes red. It was red this time, which probably meant anger was mixed with embarrassment. I did not wait to see which way the argument went, but put the tea down and said, 'I'm going for a walk.'

The air outside was beautifully cool after the masculine heat of our dining room. I smiled with relief and said out loud, 'I don't care.'

'Oh, you lovely thing,' I said to the harbour, cool and white and simple under the moon. I imagined the mangrove trees that lined the creeks humming with pleasure as the tide swelled into them. I said (this time to myself and not to the night): I don't need to stay with Dickie Pinker. I said: I thought I married a man, not a little boy. 'Hello Moon,' I said to the moon, baring my throat to her. Dickie's latest bite marks were fading and I thought the light might wash the traces away. 'Can we be friends?' – holding up my face. Then gunshots sounded on the footpath behind me. Lionel came striding along. I made room for him. He went by with his eyes fixed on where he was going, not shifting even a whisker towards his sister, his past. I watched him turn into the road running down the hill to Avondale.

'Good luck, Lionel,' I whispered, and seeing that his escape ended mine, I turned around and walked home to the man, or boy, who was my husband.

six

DICKIE SUFFERS FROM SHORTNESS OF BREATH BUT DOESN'T
let it get in the way of his morning swim. The cold shocks him.
I see rather than hear him gasp as the water reaches what he
calls, with not a trace of originality, the family jewels. That's
the point at which he dives and where my anxiety sets in. Will
he come up? There's no fun without a contest, Dickie says.
He competes with himself to see how long he can stay under.
I picture him down there, breaststroking, frog-kicking along,
his belly scraping the sand, and see his eyes bulge like snapper
eyes while his lungs strain like boilers in his chest.

Oh, Dickie, stop it, I believe in you.

If I neglect to say it – and I might one day, on purpose – his heart will give one last almighty thump down there and turn on its side for its well-earned eternal rest; and I will wade out sadly and haul my husband back to shore.

I've told him this fantasy and he loves it. He surfaces, bald headed and snorting, and sets off for Rangitoto, one hundred strokes of the Australian crawl. How can he swim and count at the same time? I sometimes count too and he's always right. When he turns and starts to side-stroke back, I relax. Not even a shark will stop him now. I wrap him in his multi-coloured towel and walk him, wheezing, shivering, home, where he stands a long while under a scalding shower, then emerges for the whisky and milk that, by God, he's earned. I never expected Dickie Pinker to be so much fun . . .

I DON'T SWIM ANY MORE BUT SOMETIMES I WALK IN THE shallows, holding a sandal in each hand and smacking their soles together when I find a rhyme that's eluded me – or, more frequently these days, when memory flashes through a door that suddenly, magically, swings open.

Here's an example: we're at the pool below the old dam on Loomis Creek. Dad has been swimming across and back, first with me and then with Roly clinging to his shoulders. Lionel doesn't need that help; he can dog-paddle across by himself. I huddle into my towel, and join him and Mum on the bank.

They're watching a girl and her boyfriend perched on a willow branch above the pool. He pushes her, she slaps him, each trying to make the other fall. The girl stands up and dives, and stays down longer than I can hold my breath. She surfaces and wipes creek water from her eyes. 'Who says you can't touch the damn bottom,' she calls.

'Mum,' Lionel whispers, 'I thought you said ladies don't swear.'

'She can't be a lady then, can she?' Mum replies.

Is that a good memory? Neutral, I think.

Here's another: Lionel makes himself an underground hut by the macrocarpa hedge. He digs a hole as deep as his shoulders, then a trench with a curve leading to the hole. He carpets them with coal sacks, and covers the hole with pieces of match-lining dragged home from a house burned down in Station Road. Other shorter bits cover the trench. Then Lionel piles dirt on top and smoothes it with the rake, and says to Dad, 'I'm going to plant radishes on top for camouflage.' He wriggles head first into the opening, and is nearly gone when Dad grabs him by the ankle and hauls him out. 'You'll suffocate in there. You need an air hole.'

'No I won't.'

'Don't argue. And dig that trench deeper or you'll get stuck.'

Lionel, grumbling, snarling, obeys. It takes a weekend to deepen the access trench. Dad finds him a piece of down-pipe and helps him fit it in a corner of the hut, where it pokes up like a chimney beyond the pumpkin patch. Lionel slides away again.

I'm not allowed in. Nor is Roly. And Lionel tells Clyde Buckley he's too big. He stays underground for hours on end. He lights a candle down there – I put my nose to the chimney and smell grease; he reads comics and smokes cigarettes made from the butts Mum and Dad squash out in their ashtrays. I smell them too but decide not to tell.

'If anyone goes in they're dead because I've got booby-traps,' Lionel says.

It's enough to keep me out, and Roly too; and Clyde Buckley really is too big.

Late one Saturday Clyde sneaked through the hedge. He blocked Lionel's entrance with dirt. Then he squatted by the chimney and lit pieces of newspaper with wax matches and poked them down the hole with a stick. He knelt and blew to keep them burning, and stuffed in more.

Dad was on the roof cleaning the gutters. He came round from the front in time to see Clyde Buckley strike a new match. Dad gave a shout. He jumped from the roof into the matchbox town Roly was building on the side lawn. I saw him flash by the living-room window and thought he'd fallen. He rolled like a gymnast and bounced to his feet and started to run. Mum and I jammed in the back door. By the time we had sorted ourselves out, Dad was charging through the potato rows, arms curved like horns, throat bellowing, and Clyde Buckley was bolting for the hedge.

Dad ripped the chimney from the ground. He knelt and yelled into the hole. Lionel's head broke through the earth five metres away. He shook dirt from his hair. Dad ran and pulled him out a second time.

'Who was it? Buckley?' Lionel cried.

'I don't want to see that boy on this section again,' Dad panted.

'I'll get him,' Lionel said, showing his broken-toothed snarl.

'You could have suffocated down there.'

'I'm all right. Where's my chimney?'

'You're not going in that hut again,' Mum said.

'It's my place,' Lionel said. 'I've got my things inside.' He knelt and started scraping loose earth away from the entrance.

Mum and Dad let him keep his hut, but when he was in residence she or I would call down the chimney at intervals: 'Are you all right?'

'Piss off,' Lionel answered me. I don't know what he said to Mum.

The hut came to its end one day when Sourface Kelly was moving his herd of cows from rented pasture at the blind end of Access Road back to his farm. The bull running with cows broke free and ran up our path and across the garden. His front legs smashed through the match-lining roof, and he lay as though sunk in a mudhole, bellowing mournfully and rolling his eyes at the sky. Kelly and his son had to dig him out.

'That's the end of it,' Dad said. 'You'd be dead if you'd been down there.'

'Yeah,' Lionel said. 'I was finished with it anyway.'

He wasn't finished with Clyde Buckley. Buckley edged his way back . . .

❅ ❅ ❅

Telephone. Damn!

❅ ❅ ❅

She's all right. Cheryl is going to be all right.

❅ ❅ ❅

RAGE AND FEAR MAKE MY HANDS SHAKE AND SEND little refluxes of sherry into my mouth. Too much sherry; I'll put it away. Dickie is off at his club. Nothing stops him. 'I can't do her any good sitting here. Are you all right, pet?' He only calls me pet when he's feeling guilty.

Her cheek is bruised where the brute punched her. One of her ribs is cracked. But the good side of her face was looking happy as we left, and not from the kisses and the strokings we gave.

There's a house – vacant possession – in Northcote with Cheryl's smiling face stapled to the fence. A man telephoned, asking to see it, and they arranged to meet at the address in half an hour. When Cheryl arrived, no one was there. She let herself in to wait for him and to see that everything was neat and clean. An empty house can look like an old whore, Cheryl says. Standing in the kitchen, wiping water stains from the tap, she heard feet padding behind her. A man wearing a hoodie came in from the hall. He saw her soft-leather bag lying on the table the owners had left behind. Cheryl thinks that saved her. She believes he lured her to the house to rape her, but her bag, supine and voluptuous, attracted him more. He grabbed at the handle, but got only one strap. Cheryl, shrieking, dived for the other and jerked him off balance over the table. With her free hand she clawed his face. ('My brave girl,' Dickie says, tears in his eyes.) He was a skeleton-handed boy with jittering eyes. As he straightened, his hoodie fell back and she saw grey tattoos climbing his throat. He let go the bag and punched her on the side of her face. Cheryl slid to the floor. She stayed on hands and knees with her head hanging, and he came round the table and kicked her in the ribs.

'He was going to rape me and then he would have killed me,' Cheryl says. The boy had conjured a knife from his pocket. ('A Maori?' Dickie asks. 'No, no, he was white. His head was shaved. He had red blotches.') He pushed her on her back, using his heel, then took a handful of her blouse and slashed it open.

'One screech and I'll cut you, bitch.'

The next-door neighbour saved her. He had seen the back-

and-forth struggle at the table, and ran out of his kitchen into the yard. He picked up a clod of earth and threw it at the window, where it exploded like a rocket. 'We've called the police,' he shouted. His wife, on the porch, was talking into a mobile phone. ('I'll take him a case of whisky,' Dickie says.) The boy, the rapist, grabbed Cheryl's bag and bolted. And before Dickie left for his club the police rang to say they'd made an arrest. 'Got the bastard,' Dickie said. 'I hope they give him one or two from me.'

He leaked tears at the hospital. I remained dry eyed, although my rage and distress equalled his and my love has always been as great. Cheryl, half-drugged, still wanted to talk, even though the swelling in her cheek had reached her mouth. A boy, she told us, with his life already lost. Compassion doesn't get beyond theory with me, and Dickie has never had much of it. Before we could find a way of disagreeing with her, the good side of her face lit up. A man carrying flowers came into the room. We did not want him there, but as Cheryl plainly did we stepped aside. He laid his flowers in her lap and took her hand.

'Tom,' she said, and tears sprang into her eyes.

'There,' he said – half of 'there, there.' He was constrained by Dickie and me at his back.

Cheryl introduced him – a fellow called Tom Quinney. (Fellow was what I felt then – I withdraw it now and replace it with nice man.) He's the one she sold an apartment to – the hard-of-hearing one not bothered by traffic noise. (He wears a hearing aid.) My thought was, He'll never do for Cheryl. My later thought is, Please let it be. In the five minutes before we left, I began to like him. He was gentle, he was firm – I mean, firm in his personality, no shifts, no vibrations, no (I think) accommodating, cushion-sinking softness, but a listening inclination to his head and an interested eye – and, as I mentioned, oh glory be!, gentleness.

'He's an ugly-looking bugger,' Dickie said in the car.

'I think she's starting to see beyond appearances.'

Tom Quinney is a tall, sandy-haired man in his fifties. He has a froggy mouth but non-froggy, wise and calculating eyes. His voice has a Southland burr and his hands, perhaps Southland farmer's hands, were wide and flat-palmed and careful with their pressure when we shook hands. Dickie likes a squeezing match. He tests his man that way. Tom Quinney understood. He gave a little grin and fought an honourable draw.

We left him to his courting and Cheryl in the happy position of being able to present a damaged face, exciting compassion, while the undamaged side stayed beautiful. But it's no joke. She could have died. All that brimming life cut and crushed; all those rich years ahead never to be. I think I would have become a mad old woman.

Now I sip sherry (just one more glass) and nibble cheese. At his club Dickie prescribes flogging and castration for that boy and his generation. Yet he did not forget to bring me a rose before he left. It's beautiful, halfway to full blown; it beams at me and molecules its scent across the room.

I love it for a moment and then I can't – the insensate thing!
It's the boy with the tattooed throat and the jittering eyes who
owns movement and intention.

seven

STEP THROUGH THE BACK DOOR OF LIONEL'S HOUSE
and you're in a graveyard overgrown with weeds. Here is the
little triangular shelf across the corner where our Philco radio
sat, bringing us the news from London and the adventures
of Speed Robinson and Jimmie Allen and The Green Hornet.
We listened to the news while eating tea at the kitchen table,
knives and forks careful on our plates, lips stitched together
while we chewed. Big Ben made his six chimes, then the man
with the sort of voice Mum wanted us to have began his
nightly conversation with her. Dad nodded his agreement with

both. For six years it was war news. Mum was sometimes in tears. The Green Hornet, Lionel's favourite, came late in the afternoon. He had a car named Black Beauty and a Japanese servant, Kato, and they drove out masked in the night to catch the crooks. Lionel sat on the floor, under the Philco. I see him wedged in the corner, arms around his knees, immoveable as a gravestone, with eyes focused backwards into his head. No one dared speak while Lionel listened.

These days that corner is stacked as high as the shelf with old newspapers and an empty vase with a broken lip sits in the radio's place.

Lionel is scalier each time I call. He's like an old lizard in his bed, with lizard claws fastened on the blanket edge. I didn't try him with memories today. My fear, my indignation, my relief still ran too high.

'He kicked her, Lionel. He broke her ribs. Then he took a knife . . .'

It brought him a little bit to life. He understands the meeting of sharp instruments with flesh. 'Little bastard. Do I know Cheryl?' he said.

'Lionel, you've met her hundreds of times. When she was a child I got you to look at her teeth. You called them neat little choppers, remember?'

His interest waned. I chattered on because that's my job. Cheryl is a subject I can do year by year – happy memories, sad ones – but soon I'm afflicted with a sense of wasting good things and also of debasing my daughter. There's a smell in

Lionel's room of things that don't have smell: eyes that don't see, skin that doesn't feel. The smell, too, of a mind closed on itself, but turning and twisting with things I can only call *things*. I timed half an hour on my watch, then made two mugs of tea and carried them into the garden, which bulges and unfurls with summer abundance.

Roly wheels a barrow down to the gate several times a week. Pumpkins, marrows, tomatoes tumble in the bottom, while silverbeet froths over the edge. He lays a neatly lettered sign on top: *Help yourself.* The neighbours do. On Friday a man comes with a van and Roly loads him up for the Saturday market in Loomis town. They share the proceeds. So my brother supplements his pension.

I told Roly about Cheryl, and that was easier. He expressed no outrage but simply went 'Tsk, tsk.' (I think that's how you spell that little tongued exclamation.) He took off his hat and let the sun beat on his white bald head. Beads of sweat stood there, clear as glass. His hat had drawn a furrow across his forehead, like the join between a red brick and a white. He blew on his tea.

It's not his fault that he doesn't know Cheryl. After one visit she has kept clear of Access Road. When I mention my brothers, she wrinkles her nose, meaning: Grotty old men. She's wrong about Roly: he's quite clean. I found him once stark naked in the garden, hosing himself free of soap suds from the crown of his head down to his ankles; and I believe he strips to the waist and washes his armpits every night at the kitchen sink. I don't know why he chooses that over the bathroom basin, where he shaves two or three times a week. Mum was particular about cleanliness.

I completed my account, puffed my indignation, contained my terror, then we sat companionably while the variegated jungle of vegetables spread before us sucked and sipped chlorophyll from the sun. (Have I got my science right? No. Never mind.) But querulousness soon broke through, as it always does at this one of my life's addresses. With Roly, my plain brother, known backwards and forwards, or so I claim, how can I not ask questions about the other? They're never new or penetrating, simply defeated. How has Lionel come to be like this?

Roly grunted and squirmed, and tipped tea dregs between his feet.

'Don't know,' he said.

It was such a characteristic response – a characterless response – that my exasperation turned on him.

'You ran away too. I haven't forgotten.'

He smiled at me. 'Is that how you see it?'

'Well, didn't you? Just a postcard at Christmas and God knows where the next one was coming from.'

'I was just doing my thing.' The idiom came awkwardly from him. He felt it too and frowned, then delivered information as if in apology: 'I was working as a gardener – parks and botanical gardens, stuff like that. You saw me doing it once.'

'I remember. You picked fruit too.'

'I did lots of things. But mainly it was gardening. It's easy enough. Just go to the council and they send you to the parks guy and you're in. I was doing that in Dunedin when I met Lionel. He was going past with a gang of his mates.'

'I never knew that.'

'I thought he might have told you.'

'Lionel never got near enough to tell me anything.'

Roly shrugged. 'I wasn't in Dunedin very long. Too cold.'

'What did he say? Did he stop?'

'He came back after.'

'By himself?'

'Yeah, by himself.' Roly grinned. 'His mates were a pretty snazzy bunch. But we had a drink in a pub. We did that a couple of times before I went up north. I went to Napier that time, I think.'

'What did he say? What did Lionel say?'

'Nothing much.'

'Oh, Roly.'

'Well, he didn't. Lionel never took much notice of me.'

'Did he have a girl?'

'I never saw one.'

My curiosity switched tracks. 'Did you?'

'Me? No. I'd better get some work done.'

'Oh, sit down, Roly. Talk to me. You're like a fish.' I meant something flapping to return to its element, but had the notion too of the sort of fish that swims away from its river birthplace into the sea and returns home only to die. Roly

walked out the gate one morning, in the dawn. This garden he
has made is his home, and he'll stay for the rest of his life. But
what happened to him out there over fifty years? If I ask, he
says he painted bridges for the Ministry of Works, he worked
as a roadman and a construction-site labourer, but mostly he
found jobs in gardens for town and borough councils up and
down the country. I see his innocent face hanging like the
daytime moon above the monotonous jobs of breaking with
a pick and dumping with a shovel, of planting and weeding
and thinning and pruning, and I want to pluck him down and
know him, not let him drift off down the sky.

'Roly,' I said, 'have you ever had a girl?'

'None of your business, Rowan.'

'What about that woman in Nelson?'

'What woman?'

'When you were in the gardens down there?'

Dickie and I made a southern trip in the seventies in an
effort – all my effort – to restore commonality to our marriage. It was no good. I remember fast driving (Dickie's sport
when no other is available), and impatience, and his question:
'Well, what do we do next?' We crossed the strait on the ferry
and drove (fast) to Nelson and ate in a café by a duck pond,
and there, across the water, saw a man pruning roses by a
fountain. He took off his hat and splashed water on his face,
and I cried – perhaps I screamed – 'That's Roly,' and dashed
out, leaving Dickie to pay.

Roly laid down his secateurs and embraced me. His jaw

rasped my cheekbone, his sweaty smell enfolded me as strongly as his arms, and when he surrendered me his hand kept a brotherly grip on mine. We sat on a bench and I fired salvos of questions, speeded up by anxiety, for Dickie was circling, looking at his watch, and amusing himself by doing quick draws and firing six-gun shots at the ducks – Dead-Eye Dick.

Roly had been in Nelson for a year. There was puzzlement in his voice at that length of time. He told me he would be leaving soon. Where did he live? A room in town. Did he cook for himself? There's a kitchen. That's the sort of answer I got. Yet his hand gripping mine was also an answer. Roly loved me. He loved us still. He was like the trees growing all around, and would behave according to his nature, grow a little each year, keep his roots deep in the soil and stay in his place – while, of course, moving about the country. He would say nothing. And he would keep on loving us. That is more than a tree can do.

'Roly, you can't go on living like this,' I said.

'Why not?'

I made a string of impatient exclamations but found no answer.

While we talked, a woman circled us. At first I thought she was strolling aimlessly, but in a moment noticed the looks she threw, full of resentment, and said to Roly, 'Is this a friend of yours?'

'Annie,' he said. 'She has her lunch with me.'

'Call her over.'

The woman sat down on his other side. I have a nose for people not right in the head. This woman, Annie, did not overlap herself; edges showed, of anxiety and need and greed and anger. She told me that Roly was in the room next door, challenging me to produce a greater closeness than that. I explained that I was his sister and hadn't seen him for a long time, thinking sister stood me aside from threatening her, but it was the opposite. Annie understood family. Perhaps she was a specialist in it. Roly put his hand on hers, stilling her agitation. I suspect touching was rare in her life, for she looked with wonderment at his brown hand in her lap.

'I'm not going anywhere, Annie,' he said. She had been a pretty woman, and underneath her fading cheeks and lined brow was pretty still, in a blurred and sepia way. She was older than Roly. She had a missing tooth and a nicotine stain in the corner of her mouth, and eyes that, tender on Roly for a moment, made a feral leap at me, then foundered on my solidity. His hand kept hers, although she tugged, and he said, 'Eat your lunch, Annie. Go on.'

Dickie was wiping duck poo from his shoe. He came towards us over the grass, dragging his foot, but stopped to kick a pine cone. He'll kick anything that lies in his path, then watch to see if it finds touch.

'Hi, Roly,' he said. 'Long time no see.'

Roly released Annie's hand and stood up. He shook Dickie's hand.

'Who's your lady friend?' Dickie said.

That was too much for Annie. She jumped up and ran away – a curious half-walking skip – leaving her lunch in a paper bag on the bench.

'What did I say?' Dickie said.

'She's not too good with people,' Roly said. He picked up the bag. 'I'd better go . . .'

Roly, leave her, I wanted to say, don't get trapped in something like that. But I hugged him, I patted him, I watched him walk away, and went with Dickie to the car and sped past the still sea out of Nelson.

'She looks as though she's been a couple of time round the block,' Dickie said.

'She's –' I said, then couldn't go on. Roly became a medium, presenting me with Annie's sorrows, and if I opened my mouth again I would weep for her.

Thirty years later, sitting beside my brother in his garden, I wanted to know what those sorrows were.

'She had a breakdown,' he said.

'What sort?'

'I don't know. Something went wonky in her head.'

'Wonky, how?'

He had no answer or, I saw, interest. Wonky was as far as his understanding went. If she had appeared at that instant, stumbling through his bean rows, he would have picked her up and comforted her, loved her in his way – but absence set his interest aside, the way switching off a radio brings silence. Roly was some new order of being. When I appeared, as I had in Nelson, and did these days in Access Road, he loved me instantly, but when I left I became barely a memory, like Annie.

'What happened to her?' I said, trying him.

'She went away. Some guy turned up. I think he was her husband.'

'Did you fight him?' I joked.

'Come off it, Rowan.'

'And what about Lionel in Dunedin, in the pub? I know why you ran away, but what about him? Did he tell you?'

Roly scrubbed his boot over the place where he'd tipped his tea dregs.

'I thought you'd know.'

'Mum, you mean? You're wrong. He loved Mum. They were like that.' I knitted my fingers together.

'It wasn't her. It wasn't Dad,' he said.

'Who then? Me?'

'No, Rowan. Everyone loves you.'

He wasn't often sarcastic. I put aside my hurt.

'Tell me, Roly.'

'He just wanted to get out of Auckland. As far as he could.'

'Dunedin?'

'He should have gone to Aussie. That might have worked.'

'Worked how? What are you talking about?'

'Ah, heck.' (Roly doesn't swear but uses a little battery of outdated exclamations.) He stood up and went to the hose, turned it a quarter on and drank from it. Sitting beside me again, he said, 'When people tell you stuff, are you meant to pass it on?'

'Yes, you are, when it's family.'

'Yeah. OK. He was getting as far as he could from Clyde Buckley.'

'Buckley? Is that what he told you?'

'He said Clyde was – loony, I guess. He did stuff that was mad.'

'Like what?'

'Dunno. Lionel didn't say. But Clyde and him used to – I don't know what it was.'

'Are you saying they were gay, doing those sorts of things?'

'No – I don't know. Getting inside each other's heads. So Lionel went to dental school to get away.'

'But he used to see Clyde when he came home. They were always together.'

'Maybe. I wasn't here.'

'As soon as Lionel turned up, Clyde was on the phone. Lionel never looked like he was running away.'

'How did he look?'

I thought about it. Buzzing, I thought. Buzzing and hard and in abeyance. On holiday in a place with corners to be turned.

'Like Clyde and he were best mates,' I said. 'There wasn't any running away. But when he started work in Christchurch he stopped coming. Mum had to go down there and see him.'

'Well –' Roly shrugged. 'I reckon they picked up girls and got in fights and drank booze. Maybe they did some stuff with drugs, I don't know. There were hardly any drugs around back then. Maybe they set fires or beat people up. Lionel said it was like walking through mud – he got drunk once and told me that. He said he was doing things he never wanted to do. But he just switched off when he got back to Dunedin. The last time I saw him down there, he told me he was never going back to Loomis again. He was graduating – don't know when it was, the end of that year? Maybe the next. He was going to get a job somewhere down south. You wouldn't want to know the names he called Loomis.'

'I'm not shockable, Roly.'

'All right. Shithole. Sorry. And that wasn't the worst.'

'I see . . . He came, though. I saw him at the dance where I met Dickie. Clyde was there too.'

'Yeah, well.' That's Roly's way of saying he's said enough. But I didn't want to let it go.

'Clyde left Loomis, didn't he? Where did he go? Not down south?'

'Whangarei. I spotted him once when I was up that way. I went past a factory door and he was in the storeroom, wearing one of those grey coats. He had a tie on too. He must have been a storeman, I guess. I took off the other way. I didn't want to see him.'

'Did he stay there?'

'Yeah, he did.'

'How do you know?'

Like every account Roly embarks on, it was simple – simple words, simple progressions of fact. Peeling them back, I'm sickened; I'm exposed in my supposition that life can be an easy sleep. I'm like a naked pupa in the ground, turned into the light by somebody's shovel.

Had I heard of Mandy Barnes? Roly asked. I'd forgotten her name, but when he reminded me, the girl with the sign reading *Tauranga or bust*, I remembered: a hitch-hiker in the late 1960s. Someone picked Mandy Barnes up and she was never seen again. The police investigation went on, the search from the turnoff at the bottom of the Bombay Hills right through to Tauranga went on month after month.

Motorists had seen her; they'd seen a green car stopping, seen a black car, seen a truck . . . It was that sort of case. Poor sad girl – she makes me cry – lying dead in a ditch somewhere, or in a swamp or a muddy river. The police had a suspect, the man in the black car. They knew it was him, but they couldn't find enough evidence and had to let him go. Nobody was ever arrested.

'The man in the black car was Clyde,' Roly said. 'His mother lived in Paeroa. He was on his way from Whangarei to see her.'

'How do you know?'

'You hear these things. Anyway, his name's in one of those books about murders that haven't been solved. The police used to watch him all the time. They probably still do.'

'But you're not saying that Lionel . . .?'

'No, not him. He lived in Christchurch.'

'Yes, yes. And he came up soon afterwards to live with Mum.'

It was like having a rotten tooth pulled out. The thing was gone – relief that rocked the mind back and forth before it settled, although a bleeding hole was left: his connection, *our* connection, with a man who had killed a girl.

'Is Clyde Buckley still alive?'

'I don't know.' Roly looked at his hands as though reminding himself of the planting and weeding they had done. 'I hope not.'

It was no casual remark. He seemed to be saying that Clyde Buckley was outside nature.

'I can look him up,' I said.

'Don't do that.' He was alarmed.

'No, I mean at the library. I don't mean see him.'

And when I left Roly, after holding him and feeling the knots of bone in his spine and the roughness of his cheek, and looking in at Lionel and saying his name and getting in response a tortoise-like half turn of his head, that's what I did: stopped at the Takapuna Library where I found *Buckley, C* in the Northland phone book, and then *Buckley, Clyde Malcolm, rtd* in the electoral roll. So he was still alive. I felt as if I'd found a jar of preserves with mould on it at the back of a cupboard. There was no other Buckley at his address. Not married, then, or she's dead. Clyde was like a hole in the ground, with nothing living near it, not a blade of grass. No spider. No slug. Nothing wants to go near Clyde Buckley.

Leave him, I thought, close the book.

I slapped the pages of the roll together and fitted it back on the shelf.

eight

DICKIE IS A TREADMILL FAILURE. IT'S ALMOST AS BAD AS missing the All Blacks.

I noticed several weeks ago that his Australian crawl was heavy armed and the stroke slower. When he came out, he stood with his hands on his knees. I draped his towel over him like a stable hand, although he's a back-paddock Clydesdale these days, and he said, 'Can't get my breath.' He also felt tightness in his chest.

I bullied him. I'm good at it, I don't stop until I get my way – so off he went to his GP, and then to the chest pain clinic for a treadmill test. Dickie would show them. He'd run a mile on the damned thing if they wanted him to.

I sat in the waiting room and he came out after half an hour, half the man who went in but spoiling for a fight all the same. There's no shortage of blood reaching his ego.

'I told you I didn't need you here,' he said.

His strained face, his poor pinched mouth, his uncertain step as he turned in a circle to find the water cooler brought me hurrying to his side. He shook off my hand.

'I can do it.'

He shuffled with his plastic cup to the nearest seat.

'What did they say, Dickie? What happened?'

'They started too fast. I wasn't ready.'

He swallowed and choked, and when he'd got his breath back said, 'I want another shot at it.'

'How long did you do?'

'Four minutes, twenty-seven seconds. That's about what a girl would do.' 'Girl' is a very bad word.

Soon a nurse led him to the cardiologist's room. She asked me if I'd like to come, but Dickie said no, so I sat for another half-hour, refusing to feel useless. I've put that behind me. I was cross that I hadn't brought my Georgette Heyer with me.

Dickie came back breathing normally. I know that bright-eyed look of intensity and anticipated triumph. The test match is all set to start, and Dickie is first five-eighths so he'll run the show, make the passes, set up the tries, kick the conversions.

OK ref, let's get started, he says.

First off there'll be an angiogram and if that shows a build-up of plaque the doctor will pump up a balloon in the artery or put in a stent, which is, as far as I can understand it, a metal tube expanding into a web. He doesn't expect to find damage to the aortal valve, but who knows? A name for what Dickie might have – he needs a name to focus his aggression on: angina. But not yet, is what I say. Shortness of breath, tightness in the chest: all you are is a treadmill failure, Dickie Pinker. Try to drink a little bit less.

We go about our lives. Dickie swims (not so far out), he goes to his club, he aims his rose gun at the roses and brings me a small perfect bloom: 'There you are, love.' I'm grateful for the whole of it, for our even days – and for Cheryl's silence with her new man. I don't want to meet him again for fear of finding imperfections.

It's two weeks until Dickie's angiogram, which will be paid for by medical insurance. It would have been four months otherwise. He could have pretended indifference, but the tightness scares him, I see it in his eyes (where's 'what the hell' gone?), and I'm afraid too. So it's, 'Why not let the buggers pay? They've screwed plenty out of us.' Jumping the queue has never bothered him.

MEMORY: THE HEART GIVES AN EXTRA BEAT AND THE graph draws a peak. You can't choose, you can't fake, you can't improve the story. Correction: you can do all three of those things and fool everyone except yourself.

Dickie worked for his father in a hardware shop in Avondale. I wanted him out of there, away from that old man (let's do some adjectives: open-pored, hairy-eared, wet-mouthed, sour-minded) who had Dickie nailed to the floor, an exhibit turning yellow and gathering dust: *My son who could have been an All Black*. I was part of Stan Pinker's disappointment. I was snooty, I couldn't cook, I left the room when he told his spotty jokes. Worse: I had taken Dickie's mind off the game. That was what caused his injury.

Dickie worked the nails free. He stepped out from behind the counter. I'd not known he had been so busy in his mind. The tide slipped out; a new tide rolled in. He worked in menswear for a while – a step up from hammers and screwdrivers and garden tools. He met different people and we started going to different parties, where I saw him glint with approval at my voice and check every now and then the expensive perm he'd bought me. He fetched me a Pimm's, stopping to talk and laugh and nod his head as he came back across the room, and I thought: What a handsome man. I had a suspicion his limp grew worse in company, reminding people of who he had (nearly) been.

I handed him his whisky and he gave me the Pimm's.

'Rowan,' he said softly, 'see that joker over by the chicken legs.'

I looked and saw a jolly man with grease on his chin.

'Yes.'

'He's a millionaire.'

'Well, good for him.'

Dickie smiled happily. 'He makes tennis rackets and cricket bats, stuff like that. Imports them too. He's a nice guy. Not stuck up. I sold him that shirt.'

'It's too tight on him.'

'Yeah, I know, but he wanted it that size. Dunno why. A millionaire, eh?'

'Jolly good.'

I was beginning to understand that I didn't like these parties, because there was so much talk and no talk at all. I did not like having permed hair.

Ten minutes later, Dickie nudged me. 'See that joker coming in from the balcony? He's a millionaire too.'

So I learned Dickie's new ambition.

'What from?'

'Eh? Fish. Doesn't matter what from.'

Dickie made his money – our money – in paper. He borrowed from his father and went in with a sharp young fellow called Ron Stock. Stock & Pinker, Paper Products: paper in reams, paper in pads, in exercise books, in single sheets; paper napkins, toilet paper, paper hats, paper streamers, wrapping paper, Christmas cards; Stock & Pinker cards for every anniversary Dickie and Ron were able to dream up. They'd have made paper motor cars if it had been possible. And pretty paper girlfriends for the private enjoyment of clever young new-minted millionaires.

It was hard not to enjoy Dickie's pleasure and delight. It was hard not to admire the energy he poured into his work, the hours he put in, the travelling, the driving through the night, the flight connections made and the meetings that ended in new deals. Dickie dummied, he sidestepped, he ran for the line and dotted down between the posts.

I watched for a while. Then I turned my back and walked away to save myself. He wanted me to be what I couldn't be, the person he described as 'my wife'. He was doing his job, and wife was mine. I must wear smart clothes; I must have my hair done, and my nails, and learn make-up, and have his friends to dinner and not laugh so loud. There was no need to learn cooking: we could get someone in to look after that.

Not laugh so loud? Dickie was losing himself. I had not seen it properly until he said that. I'd been seeing him as a caricature and getting enjoyment from it, of a fragile kind, while building my worried notion of superior worth. Now I saw the danger he was in.

I pleaded with him. 'Dickie, we've got Cheryl, isn't she enough? Dickie, don't throw our marriage away.' And much more – all of which he shook his head at angrily. Dickie had made himself a new set of needs, and mine seemed to match none of them. Even Cheryl was invisible to him, except in the half-hours he was able to find for her.

I exaggerate. There were holidays, but Dickie was either blank eyed, calculating paper enlargements of himself, or else he was larger than life to fill in the time.

I missed him. I grieved for him. But also I was hard. Cheryl's future equipped me with an iron stare, and my illness taught me the need for iron choices in dangerous times.

In the beginning I'd had miscarriages. Then Cheryl came. I've never kept a photo album but display pictures in my head: Cheryl in her bassinette, Cheryl on her tummy on a rug, Cheryl at the wave's edge stepping back from the foam, Cheryl screwing her fists into her eyes the way tired babies do, as if trying to force them back into her head. All those and more, many more. I have no presence except as the air surrounding her. Dickie appears now and then.

Our second baby, five years after Cheryl, was stillborn. Dickie blubbered and I held him tight. His loud grief matched the silent end of part of my life. I refuse now to think about that child. Dickie insisted we call him Leon. Leon lived his whole life inside my body, and my body grieved for many years. But it was long ago and the pain is diffused, and I call the stabs of ageing in my feet and knees and ribs Leon pains. It's not possible to stay pure. Humour is a ramshackle cart, carrying me away from loss.

Several years after that, I lost all future babies. I'm not going to dwell on it. There are two words I hate: fistula, hysterectomy. I've written them down, that's enough. I saw my husband's incomprehension, so kept the details to myself, as he wished. He patted me a lot. He said, 'Does it hurt?' He said, 'Poor Rowan.' He said, 'How long before you can come back to me?' – meaning sex. In my heart I said, Never. I did not hate Dickie, did not even dislike him; he simply failed to register most of the time. I saw how his mind arranged the facts: things had gone wrong in the female part of my body so it was up to me to deal with them in the female part of my mind. He would have described that as 'fair'. (By God, he had his work to do and it took everything out of him.) All right, fair, I agreed. And fair that he should become paper thin to me.

So I freed myself from my marriage while continuing to share house, time, money, entertainments with Dickie; share Cheryl too, when he could fit her in. I became scrawny in my emotions (except for Cheryl) and physically scrawny as well, and pale skinned (no make-up) and bushy haired (no perm). I had no fat on me, body or mind, but was aware somewhere in my midriff of a hollow shaped like a pudding bowl, and shiny like a bowl or like overstretched skin, where an affective part had been removed.

I was no wife to Dickie for many years, poor man. I don't think divorce ever entered his head. Embedded in his notion of manhood was loyalty, and at the centre of loyalty the magic name: my wife. Dickie began growing up when he was able to use those words. They gave him a different kind of weight than rugby had promised, the kind adults feel. But these are things I cannot put my hand on easily. All I'll say is that breaking 'man and wife' apart would stab splinters into Dickie's idea of himself.

He was deeply hurt. He believed he gave me everything

I could want. It bewildered him and made him savage that I turned away, and it gave him the right to turn away from me and follow the instructions of his blood. Simply put, Dickie had women. I don't blame him in the least.

That time seems like dirty water splashed on the floor. Although it has dried, a stain is left, with edges but no recognisable shape. I step around it carefully when I notice, but mostly tread across unaware.

Dickie's women were less important than the loss of the friendly connections we used to have. I spoke with the longest-serving of them once, a pleasant-looking woman, over-painted but not by much, and was surprised to find her bitter and shrill. She could not understand why Dickie would not leave me. I told her I didn't mind her having him but what she'd get would never be more than half.

'You're cruel. How can a man like Dickie stay with you?' she wept.

I was, in fact, more than one woman at that time. Mistaking bitterness for a genre, I wrote little paragraphs describing how ill used I was. But several of them got away from me and turned into stories. I keep them with my poems in a folder in the bottom of my undies drawer, where Dickie never goes. One or two are not bad. Here's the best of them. I'll paste it in, so turn the page.

❖ ❖ ❖

MOTHER'S HOLIDAY

'You had better ring for a taxi,' Anna Worth said briefly. She had ceased her slow pacing of the kitchen and was leaning her uncomfortable weight against the deal table.

John Worth reached for his hat and came round the room to face his wife. 'I'm sorry for this, Anna,' he said, his voice roughly sympathetic. With instinctive tact he withheld his customary kiss and let himself quietly out into the night.

Like a figure in a tableau the woman at the table remained motionless. Inwardly she was mustering strength for the age-old ordeal; only then did she give voice to her pain and fear. 'Will I never get used to this?' she exclaimed impatiently. 'Never –' the word seemed to mock her; 'Never!' Anna Worth's babies had all, at their appointed times, arrived in the still hours of the night. 'Moon moths fluttering in by night light,' she had once, in a serene moment, described them. Her fifth child promised to be no exception to this nocturnal rule.

The town clock was striking twelve, when the taxi, with its somewhat tense and shaken occupants, swept up to the curb at the hospital entrance. Spry with relief, the driver took Anna's suitcase and hastened to deposit it in the open door-way. Back in his seat, he lit a cigarette with relish, watched his fare disappear, mused for a moment on the strangeness of life, then deftly spun his car away and out on its return journey. In sudden appreciation of his carefree bachelorhood he began to sing to the accompaniment of his thrumming tyres.

In the white-lit hospital corridor, Anna was looking at John. The great stone building about and above them seemed empty of all sound, hushed in a midnight silence. The night nurse, on rubber-shod feet, had gone to wake the matron.

Anna, experiencing a curious moment of awareness, saw her husband as a complete stranger, about whose positive self she knew nothing. His face, in the harsh light, appeared to have taken on new and deeper lines. Presently he would go, and she would be left to bring his child into the world. He would go, his strong, free body untouched by her travail; soon he would be comfortably bedded in his sister's suburban home, and she, Anna—

'Will you please come this way?' the night nurse called down the corridor length.

'Good-night, Anna – good-night, girl.' John Worth patted his wife's shoulder. He stood irresolute for one awkward moment and then, with much unsaid, he left her abruptly. Watching him go, Anna felt a sudden tug of pity for him; his inability to aid her even by word of mouth. 'Men are such babies,' she thought appropriately.

THERE WAS A CLOCK IN THE LABOUR ROOM; A SMALL, implacable-faced clock that stood on a locker top. Anna, prostrate now, and nearing her 'big moment', could follow the slow, slow progress of its hands. As each wave of pain caught and carried her, she sought its round face desperately. 'Soon,' she kept praying silently. 'Soon now, soon!'

The matron, a sister and a nurse were whiling away the in between minutes discussing golf. Grimly Anna lay listening to their trivial enthusiasms. 'They have waited at this table often enough,' she thought, 'but they have never yet waited on it! No wonder they can talk golf!' She moaned uneasily and at once the matron was beside her.

'Now —' the efficient voice commanded. Anna felt a firm hand against her back, she gathered her strength valiantly, but as the old, old agony, so hardly borne, gripped her body she turned over convulsively.

'Back now!' the matron ordered sharply and slapped Anna's bare buttock, much as the farmer slaps the rump of a refractory cow! Hot humiliation flooded Anna's distressed mind. 'I'll not forget that slap,' she vowed breathlessly.

At two o'clock she asked for chloroform. The matron fitted the thrice-blessed gauze mask to her patient's perspiring nose and hurriedly sought the container which held that most goodly of gifts to mankind — chloroform. During the final long breath of relief it brought to Anna her baby was born — so suddenly and swiftly as to surprise the four women in the theatre, Anna most of all. Soft as down she felt it lying against her upper thigh, her baby, already in its first scarce-breathing moment, a treasure beyond price.

'What is it?' Anna asked weakly.

'A girl,' said the matron, with calm satisfaction, and proceeded to call for the tiny being's first cry.

'You can talk golf now,' Anna said thoughtlessly – and closed her heavy sleep-starved eyes. She was tired! tired! tired! but gladly so. Somewhere in this big grey hospital there was a warm bed waiting for her – and in the nursery there would be a cot for her baby, a cot with 'Worth' printed on its white tag; one cot among many, and to Anna, by far the most important cot.

'THERE'S A BREATHLESS HUSH IN THE WARD TONIGHT!' Anna misquoted. She was sitting up in her bed, titivating, as were two of her ward mates. It was visiting hour again; at least three dutiful husbands were scheduled to tiptoe (instinctive habit) into the ward. Anna glanced covertly to the corner bed on her right hand. On it lay an outsize in women, huddled beneath her covers. For two days this fat girl had lain face to the wall, a bundle of dejection. Anna knew she was a childless mother, her baby having been stillborn; she suspected too that the unhappy girl was also husbandless, although on her plump left hand she wore a bright gold wedding ring.

'Poor girl,' thought Anna, 'she has no baby, and something tells me, no husband either. And to be on a starvation diet, too – no wonder she's always weeping under her blankets.'

The two more fortunate of Anna's companions were eagerly discussing a plan to outwit the sister on duty should their husbands bring forbidden dainties into the ward.

Suddenly the squeak of a man's boots sent a thrill of

anticipation through the ward. Three pairs of eyes turned hopefully towards the door. Through it a thick-set man was peering short-sightedly, discomfort and doubt reddening his heavy face. In one hot hand he was gripping a bunch of wilted, mixed flowers.

'Is Jesse McDoo in here?' he asked, catching Anna's friendly eye.

There was a sudden movement in the bed on Anna's right.

'Dad!' the fat girl was crying. 'Dad! Oh, Dad!'

Presently, from behind the screen that the man adjusted round his daughter's bed, Anna heard his first whisper: 'Your Mum don't know I'm here.'

Anna lay back on her pillows and pulled the blankets up around her ears. She felt she would rather guess the fat girl's story than hear it by eavesdropping. 'Bless the man for a kind father,' she breathed thankfully. And then John Worth walked in, and everyone's story but her own became unimportant.

The long ward was a-buzz with whispered conversations. Secretive screens were round the four beds. The three babies had been brought in on the arm of the obviously bored nurse and distributed one to each bed. Anna, with her precious bundle propped up on her knees, looked at her husband.

'She's a beautiful baby,' she said.

'All your babies have been beautiful, Anna,' John Worth complimented quietly.

'All our babies,' Anna corrected, and smiled into his sincere eyes.

'Lights out in ten minutes,' the bored nurse called from the doorway. 'This baby racket is bunk!' she grumbled impatiently to herself. Outside the hospital her fiancé was waiting for her.

* * *

I LIKE THAT. I MANAGED TO STEP OUTSIDE MYSELF INTO other lives, trailing no more than bits of anger and disappointment. My failure to write more stories about that Anna who is not me, and find other fat girls, is part of the stain I step around.

Oddly enough, Dickie and I still enjoyed each other. I don't mean in bed, although that too made a stop-and-start new beginning not long after the shrill woman departed, bearing gifts (and wearing them), from Dickie's life. I mean I enjoyed knowing him and not being barred from the rooms of self-delight he inhabited; and enjoyed all his stumbles and shouts of rage; his delusions of importance; his open pleasures and feeble lies, and the way he swelled himself with victories – he needed one each day, even if it was no more than winning a twenty-dollar bet with one of his mates. All these things added up to Dickie. In many ways I preferred him to John Worth. With John Worth I had one foot trapped in my former self – one foot in a bog. Dragging free took time, although the fat girl, hidden under blankets, and her father creaking along the ward meant I was making progress. But when I was free and held myself firmly by the hand, I grew lazy. Rediscovering Dickie seemed enough – yet he's such a simple organism, how could that be? Is he my victory or defeat?

He came straggling back, bringing more of himself each time, and I made matching efforts, with clothes and hair, so that he need not be ashamed of me. We set up house in Kohimarama, back from the beach, and set up our marriage again, and endured bumpy times and enjoyed smooth ones, and fitted beside each other into a life that satisfied us like a meal continually interrupted. I mean our stomachs rumbled and our taste buds were not right, but we finished with coffee and a liqueur, then strolled in the garden, sniffing the night flowers and admiring the moon.

I'm diminished, I know it, but I gave my agreement to becoming the person I am. So no complaints. Dickie is my companion. I have no complaints about him either.

His business prospered. He joined the fish man and the cricket-bat man – a millionaire, which doesn't mean today what it meant back then, so, a millionaire several times over. (My father would have called him rich and my mother wealthy.) Then he surprised me. I had thought he was enjoying himself and would go on, but I had forgotten he was playing a game, playing to win, and games come to an end. Somewhere in the jumble of aggressions and enjoyments that fill his mind, Dickie heard the referee blow full time. He raised his arms in triumph and plodded from the field.

In his long retirement we have become less 'wealthy'.

Dickie could never work up interest in investing his money. He put it here and put it there, grumbling that it wasn't work and, I could see, thinking that it wasn't any sort of contest either. We lost quite heavily in the 1987 crash; but never mind, Dickie says, we've still got plenty. 'Let those silly bastards play their games,' he says, which makes me giggle. So we go on.

From Kohimarama we shifted to a beachfront house in Takapuna, and then to a smaller one back from the beach, where we found roses in bloom. Cheryl had her troubles, her marriage and children and divorce, and we dreamed for her, planned for her all the happy futures she could not find for herself – but she went her way. Dickie played golf, then took up bowls. We travelled a lot. My writing turned into a search for rhymes and my reading into Georgette Heyer, whom I love although she's absurd. I'm absurd, too, in my way; but I like the direction I'm facing, not left or right, not up or down, just with my eyes wide open, hoping to see a few steps ahead, see a little part of the way I'll go.

I've said enough. This is where we are: a house, a garden, a troubled daughter, absent but happy (I hope) grandsons, our pastimes, our money in the bank. We also have our memories, though I don't think Dickie goes there much.

nine

NO MATRON SLAPPED MY BOTTOM. MY MOTHER WAS
the one in that ward. She dressed the woman down in her
private-school voice, then had to turn her anger into getting
Roly born. The girl with the stillborn baby was also there.
I made her fat, poor soul, and invented her father. My own
father explained to me why boots creak, but that was too
much detail for my story.

He worked in the same factory all his life and rose to fore-
man at the end. With the extra money he bought one of
those vans with the body made of wood, and drove it badly,

woodenly, along the western roads and out to the beaches, with Mum on a cushion beside him, limousining. In our own limousine we purred along behind. Watching Dad, enjoying him, slowed Dickie down.

I said, 'Why don't we buy them a proper car?'

'My old man would take one. Yours wouldn't,' Dickie said.

He gave him bottles of whisky instead, and for the last few years of his life Dad drank only the best.

That van (a Bradford, Dickie reminds me), lovingly maintained, kept puttering along for many years, and died with Dad. He drove to work that Friday morning. On the Whau Creek bridge outside New Lynn a horse float on its way home from the Avondale racecourse broke its coupling and ran into the oncoming traffic, where it cracked the Bradford open, tore its panelling like paper, and killed my father instantly.

People kept reminding me that he didn't suffer, but my real comfort came from Dad's life: his honesty, his simplicity, and all those correlations between mind and hand bespeaking love. I felt him choke with it as he picked me up after a fall, sponged my bleeding knee, swabbed my elbow and wiped my tears away with his handkerchief (not always clean). How did he feel after whipping the boys? Mum told me he went into the garden and was sick. I'm sure that didn't happen every time – but were there so many times? Mum reddened my bottom with the hearth brush frequently, but Roly tells me he can remember only two or three hidings – 'which I asked for,' he says. Lionel had more. He asked for them too. But poor Dad. Love marked the boundaries of his natural world. Duty came from the encroaching dark.

He died. (The horse in the horse float died too.) My mother stayed with Dickie and me for a while – we were still in Kohimarama – but went back to Te Atatu Road when she and I began to bark and snarl at each other. Visiting her, I pulled in my extensions and became her daughter, while she (thin and weepy one moment, savage the next, when staying with me) put out feelers in every room, finding how to fill them and who she would be.

That, it turned out, was a smiley widow with a sentimental view of the past, a persona that left her incomplete. It was some time before I discovered her two lost boys made up the rest. She saw them as not only lost to her – she could perhaps have borne that – but lost to themselves: Roly the postcard man, labouring in gardens here (up north) and there (down south), unmarried still and needing nothing and having nothing, and growing old with his life not lived; and Lionel in Christchurch, unmarried too, communicating by phone once a month and saying only that he was well. She did not believe it. Lionel worried her most.

I drove out to see her with a gift, my newest poem:

Little mother melancholy, I suspect your heart
Of holding grievous converse in which I have no part . . .

She read it and said, 'It's lovely, Rowan,' and handed it back.

'No, it's for you.'

'I'm not little,' she said, patting her stomach, trying to joke.

'You're getting littler every day,' I said. 'Please tell me.'

'I'm all right. I'm missing your dad.'

'Yes, I know. But he doesn't worry you, does he? It's the boys.'

'No. They came to the funeral. I thought they'd come more often, that's all.'

'They've got their lives, Mum.'

'No they haven't. They haven't got lives.'

At the funeral service she had freed her hand from Roly's to brush tears from her cheeks, and Lionel had given her his handkerchief, folded square and white as ice. Now she cried properly, with her head laid on the table, and I put mine beside it in the crook of her arm and tried to comfort her, but in the end cried too.

When we talked there were many words but little to say. I argued for Roly – he had chosen his life and it made him happy – but could not argue for Lionel. His choice, his way, when I thought of it, seemed clean and arid, a germ-free life. It was easy to fill in dentist things – basins and masks and rubber gloves and drills – and leave him in his surgery with a white nurse for company, and not wonder about what went on when he locked the door at night and headed home; but Mum's tears and mine put an end to that.

'What's wrong with him, Rowan? What's wrong?'

'I don't know. He's got some sort of knot tied inside him. I don't know.'

'Why won't he get married? He used to have girls.'

'He doesn't like sharing his money,' I joked.

'He's not mean. He sends me cheques. He sent Dad cheques. He has for years.'

'How much?'

'None of your business, Rowan. What do you mean, knots? What sort of knots?'

'I just mean he's tied to a post.' I can come out with metaphors on demand but they're no diagnosis. Mum needed someone to explain Lionel in plain terms and tell her what she should do.

I drove out to see her every second or third day, and was with her when she phoned him on the night of his birthday. Lionel was fifty, a number she felt must produce a change.

'Lionel, it's your mother. Happy birthday, Lionel.'

There was no extension so I could not listen in, but his voice had an edge like glass and I heard him almost as clearly as Mum.

'Hello, Mum. I thought you might ring.'

'What are you doing, Lionel? Are you having a party?'

'Me? No. I'm watching TV.'

'Oh Lionel, on your birthday. When you're fifty.'

'Don't remind me. Sixty next stop.'

So they went on. He hadn't had anything special for dinner

but was drinking whisky and watching *Antiques Roadshow*.

'You should have your friends there, Lionel. Did the people at work give you something?'

'They didn't know. Birthdays are –' he deleted 'crap' '– no big deal.'

'Oh, but fifty. Lionel, did you get my present?'

'Sure. Very nice. Thank you, Mum.' He hurried on, concealing that he hadn't unwrapped it. 'Tell you what, I'll cancel some appointments, I'll come up and see you, maybe next week. How would that be?'

'Oh, Lionel, wonderful. That would be wonderful. We'll have a party for you here.'

'No, no parties. Just you and me. I'll rent a car and take you on some drives.'

'That would be wonderful. We could drive along the Scenic Drive. Lionel, Rowan's here. I'll put her on.'

'No, no, just tell her hello. Is pea-brain with her – what's his name?'

'No, Richard isn't here.' She smiled at me, pretending Lionel had said something nice. I drifted into the kitchen and sat at the table. I was pleased with Lionel. Mum would be happy for a while.

I drove out and had lunch with them while he was visiting, and found him friendly, even affectionate, and younger-looking, fresher-looking than I'd expected. I'd thought he would show some sort of desiccation. His eyes, so used to peering, seemed to take in whole persons, especially Mum, and his voice had none of the sharp-filed edge it had on the phone. He was wiry in his wrists and, I imagined, inside his clothes, and quick with his movements in a flicking way, although he slowed down when close to Mum, as though she exercised a restraining force. Her doubts and worries were gone, if only for the duration. She was, in fact, tired with happiness.

After lunch she lay on her bed for a nap. Lionel and I walked down the hill into Loomis. I had to slow him down, and he told me that he worked out in a gym and had run several half marathons.

'You never told us.'

He looked surprised. 'I didn't think you'd be interested. You look pretty fit yourself.'

We talked inconsequentially until I asked about Roly.

'Good old Roly. He keeps in touch,' Lionel said.

'That's more than he does with me. Where is he now?'

'Somewhere in Wellington last time I heard. I'll know when I get a phone call.'

'He phones?'

'Sure. We talk. We're brothers, Rowan. Hey, I'm sorry, you're our sister too.' He touched my shoulder. 'But you've got – Dick.'

The pause annoyed me. 'Why haven't you got someone? You could have a wife.'

He contracted his shoulders – I remember it like the sliding of oiled plates in a machine, one over the other, consolidating its strength.

'No need, Rowan,' he said in his clicking voice.

'Of course there's a need . . .'

'Sure. I pay. There are some nice clean gentlemen's clubs in Christchurch. They even have back doors if you don't want anyone seeing.'

'Well,' I said, 'I'm glad you get some pleasure.'

'But, you know –' he suddenly grinned: beautiful teeth '– working out at the gym is pretty good too.' The grin didn't reach his eyes. He closed them, but not before I'd seen something lost, and angry too, and – is it possible? – a narrative as well, Lionel's life, which I had no time to grasp before he snapped his head away and cried, 'Hey, Access Road. Let's not go down.'

'Why not?'

'Ancient history, Rowan. Let's look at the school.'

'That's ancient history, too.'

'Maybe. But I had a pretty good time there.'

So we looked at the school, ambled in the playgrounds, without any throb of emotion. A teacher put her head out a window and asked what we wanted. I explained that we'd gone there as children, but although polite she was unimpressed. We went away, walked down the rest of the hill and peered from the bridge at the shrunken creek, then climbed back to Te Atatu Road, where I handed Lionel over to Mum and drove home with part of my worry lifted away but a snaky feeling under my heart. I could not believe in him. What was the story he had given me no time to read?

He flew to Christchurch the next day, and a week later Mum phoned excitedly: 'Rowan, I've just had a call from Lionel. He wants to come up and live with me.'

My first thought was, That's mad. My next was, He wants to lie down, he's had enough.

'You mean for good?' although there was no mistaking it.

'There's part of a practice he can buy in Loomis. He had a look at it when he was here. I didn't know.'

Lionel working neatly, ticking things off. I began to feel he had it in his nature to change; alter the seating arrangements in himself, put this stiff but comfortable chair in a different corner where it would catch a little more sun, and sit up straight in it with his hands on his knees and smile at the person across the room where there had been no person for twenty years or more.

He needs her, I thought, and he'll be careful. I did not want him using Mum and hurting her. I overlooked that he might come to love her.

On the night she phoned me, she said wistfully, 'He might find some nice woman up here,' but after he'd lived with her a while Mum stopped hoping for that. She wanted Lionel for herself. I've no doubt he found another gentlemen's club and paid a visit when the need was urgent, but for almost twenty years he sat at home with her, the pair of them in a kind of cream and honey stasis. Sometimes it was nice to see; sometimes it made me sick. This was the way Victorian spinsters lived with Papa. There was nothing wrong with it – a home, a hearth, two lonely people keeping each other company – but little right for the one weighted down with a life unlived.

After several years Lionel confounded me by buying a piano, taking up the lessons he had started as a boy and playing tunes with scarcely a note wrong. (He was good at Handel's *Largo*.) He took Mum to concerts; he taught her to drink wine; he made her happy, and was happy too – yet sometimes he made me think of a dog that has been beaten and found a new home where there's food and affection, almost enough to cancel fear.

Food there was. Mum learned to cook. No more lamb's fry baked into paving stones. No more cabbage boiled to a yellow sludge. For the first time since she had left school she studied, even though it was only recipe books. All the things she had turned away from in her married life, sometimes with horror, appeared on her table: olives, oysters, paté, sour cream, smelly cheese. She cooked Italian, Swedish, French; she baked whole fish; she baked bread and muffins and Eccles cakes and puddings of every sort. My mother whose sole treat for her children had been date roll was able in her old age to make a perfect crème brûlée.

Lionel lost his edges. Food was only a part of it. Love and care, admiration, moulded him like hands; habits and routines enfolded him. He sat on the sofa smiling like a cat. Cat now? I said dog before, and hints of a dog that had been starved and beaten remained in the turning of his eye, showing too much white, in a fawning laugh like the wagging of a tail. But mostly he was still and contented. He and Mum read books together; he drove her into Auckland to the pictures and took her to dinner in restaurants. At home they became devotees of *Coronation Street* and talked about the characters like people from next door. Several times, hearing Lionel say Ken or Deirdre, I found myself thinking, Good, he's making friends, until Mum replied, 'She's getting wrinkles. They should use more make-up on her.'

Roly made half a dozen visits but stayed only a night or two before vanishing back into postcard land. Mum seemed happy to let him go. She waved from the door, and Roly walked off almost in the way he had left as a boy. I wished he would visit me, but all he did was telephone to say hello. I put my phone down once, and rushed across and caught him in the hallway as he shouldered his duffel bag. So I got a hug.

'Roly's such a good boy,' Mum said. 'I just wish he'd made more of himself.'

It seemed to me that Roly had made a great deal: a man who was contented and knew who he was.

I telephoned him when he was living in Te Kuiti. 'Roly,' I said. 'I'm coming to see you. Book me in at a hotel.'

'No need,' he said. 'I've got a mattress.'

I drove down not knowing why, except that it was time to fix him in my mind after a gap of more than three years; and indeed I did not know him for a moment, with his balding head and mottled beard. He was a handyman, an elementary fix-it man for the town council, nailing broken railings and unblocking drains. He lived in a tiny council flat, where my mattress proved to be no more than that. (I'd thought he meant bed. What's that figure of speech we learned at school? I've looked it up: synecdoche, part for the whole.) He laid the yellow leaking thing between two chairs in the living room and slid a cushion into a pillowslip and gave me two blankets, depriving himself of one. This, after a dinner which we walked out to buy: two meat pies from a dairy. It was just as well I'd brought a bag of muffins from Mum.

We watched TV on a tiny set – it might even have been black and white – then I slept badly, tormented by lumps in the mattress and Roly's snoring from his bedroom. Weetbix for breakfast, then Roly went off to work and I drove home, resting every hour or so and once snoozing with the seat re-clined. I was happy. I was pleased with this Roly who was solid set, steady eyed, scar handed, loud in his laugh, slurping with his tea (all sorts of attributes he had), after the careful brother who lived with Mum.

❋ ❋ ❋

RECENTLY I CAME ACROSS A CARTOON IN A BOOK, showing a sad, plain woman with haunted eyes curled up against a headstone in a cemetery. The caption read: *Mother loved me but she died*. A cruel cartoon in which I saw Lionel.

It's not the whole story of course. They watched television until half-past nine that night, then Lionel switched off the set. Mum had not been feeling well. He put out his hands to haul her to her feet, but she said, 'I'll just sit a minute longer.' Then she sneezed loudly, widened her eyes with (Lionel said) a kind of astonishment, and fell sideways on the sofa. These tiny explosions in the head that wipe out a world. Mum never regained consciousness but died in hospital next day.

Lionel held himself together at the funeral and for several years after. He stayed on in the house. Mum, always fair, had left third shares to Roly and me. Lionel bought us out. He lived alone. He had no need for a brother or sister. He did not bother to tell us when he sold his practice in Loomis. He did not tell us that he'd bought the house in Access Road.

ten

DICKIE'S ANGIOGRAM SHOWED 'ARTERIES LIKE AN ALL Black forward'. That was a clever thing for the doctor to say. Dickie glowed with satisfaction as the orderly trolleyed him back to bed. 'Beat the buggers,' he told me, meaning that he'd beaten his poor old heart.

He wanted to go straight home, get to the club, tell his tale, but the blood-thinning medication he takes to ward off strokes made him bleed through the hole the angiogram tube had made in his groin. The nurse let him walk to the toilet instead of using a bottle and, coming back, the front of his gown was suddenly sprayed with red. Fright and enjoyment: which did he feel more? He loved the colour of his blood. He liked it when the nurse spent ten minutes pressing her clenched fist in his groin. He chatted with her, bluff and brave, while I sat in the corner, cancelled out.

What is wrong with him then? Why the breathlessness? The doctor thinks maybe something gastric and has given him pills. I think old age and stupidity. Dickie lied on the hospital form. Alongside the question about alcohol intake he wrote *moderate*.

He has a purple bruise from his groin down to his knee. He made me photograph it. I might give it to him, framed, on his next birthday.

WE HAD CHERYL AND TOM TO DINNER TO CELEBRATE. Cheryl's bruise has gone and her loose teeth have set in her gums. There's still some pain from her cracked rib. The boy who attacked her is remanded in custody, and she hopes they'll give him drug counselling while he's inside, and psychological counselling and, 'Oh God, some lessons in decent behaviour.'

Tom laughed and said, 'Of course they won't.'

It turns out Tom was a policeman, starting as a constable in Invercargill, where he was born, and working his way into criminal investigation, where he rose to the rank of detective inspector. In his early fifties, just a year or two ago, he perfed

– a word I had to have explained. His wife was dead, his parents dead, his children married. A health scare (he was okay now, he winked at Cheryl) made him think about where he was going. To Nelson, he decided, to the sun. But he lasted less than a year there. He'd spent his life in provincial cities, why move to another? Nelson, he said, was walking by the river feeding the ducks. Cutting stale bread into cubes one morning, he thought, Do I want to spend the rest of my life doing this? He sold his apartment, got in his car, crossed the strait on the ferry and headed north. He would try our biggest city and see if size would jolt him on to a new path.

'It seems to be working,' he grinned.

I wondered what he did for money – the apartment Cheryl had sold him wasn't cheap – but didn't ask. Later in the evening, in the sitting room with coffee, he mentioned that he'd got a half-share from the sale of the farm where he'd grown up. So that's Tom: a very nice man, and he'll do for Cheryl. She thinks so too.

I asked him cheekily if he'd been a good policeman.

'Sure, I was good,' he said. 'I knew my job.'

'Did you catch any murderers?' Dickie said.

'I worked on one or two homicides, yeah.'

'Oh, don't tell us,' Cheryl said.

'Did you ever hear of a man called Clyde Buckley?' I don't understand how I came to ask.

Tom looked at me with interest – with a change in the density of colour in his eyes. 'That was Whangarei. I've heard of him. He's still POI.' Another explanation needed: person of interest.

He asked me how I'd heard of Buckley, but I drew back. I felt as if I'd let cold air into the room and taken the warmth off this man I wanted for my daughter.

'More coffee anyone?' I said.

'Have you met the guy?' Tom said.

'Not for more than fifty years. Don't talk about him.'

'You knew him when you were a kid?'

'No. Yes. He lived two streets away. But he was older. I never knew him.'

'Who is he? What did he do?' Cheryl asked.

'Killed a girl,' Tom said. 'At least we think he did. She was hitch-hiking down on the Hauraki Plains. Someone saw her getting picked up in a Morris Oxford. The driver was putting her pack in the boot. He was a guy with a pot belly and long arms.' Tom laughed, 'Some description.' But to me long arms was horribly accurate. 'Some car, too. You know how many Morris Oxfords they had back then? And maybe it was blue and maybe black.'

'So how did you get on to the guy?' Dickie said.

'Not me, I was in Timaru. They got him, but they couldn't make a case, not enough to stand up anyway. The file's still there. They have a look every year or two.'

'Like Mona Blades and Jennifer Beard,' Dickie said.

'Yeah, like them. Except the guy we liked for Jennifer Beard died a couple of years ago. I worked on that one.'

'So how did they finger Buckley?' (Dickie likes using words like 'finger' but usually gets the meaning wrong. Tom grinned at him. They're going to get on.)

'They couldn't find a car and they couldn't find a body. They dragged every creek and drainage ditch on the plains. Then after three months a farmer pulled her body out of a swamp over by Raglan.'

'I remember that one,' Dickie said. 'Some kid had a photo of a car down at the beach. One of them was . . .'

'A black Morris Oxford. They could just read the licence plate. So up to Whangarei and this guy Buckley –' Tom laughed '– a man with a pot belly and long arms.'

'So why didn't you lock the bastard up?'

'They tried hard enough, but they couldn't make a case that the legal boys would buy. Buckley didn't have the car any more. He sold it to a kid who ran it into a creek. By the time they pulled it out . . .' Tom shrugged. 'Lucky Mr Buckley. He said he never picked up hitch-hikers. Couldn't shake him on that. And no positive ID, so –' Tom spread his hands '– no case. It was close, though. They bring him in and ask him questions now and then, keep the bugger jumping, but he's got his story off pat. He doesn't change a word . . .' Tom looked at me. 'What was he like as a kid?'

I told him about Clyde Buckley trying to suffocate Lionel in his underground hut.

'A psychopath. Yeah, psychopath,' Dickie said. 'I hope you gave him a bloody good thumping while you had him.'

Tom only grinned at him, a little less friendly now.

'Getting him into court was what mattered. If it had been my case – well, wouldn't have made any difference. The guys on the job, they couldn't get that last little bit.'

'So what do they think happened? What's the theory?' Dickie said.

Tom glanced at me, then at Cheryl. 'You want to know?'

'I do,' Dickie said.

Tom shrugged. 'It goes like this. He drove into a side road and did whatever he did. Then he put her body in the boot with her pack and drove to Paeroa and spent the night with his mother.'

'With the girl still in the boot?' Cheryl cried.

'That's what they think. When they asked him why he went across to Raglan next day, he said he'd had enough of his mother and he still had a couple of days off work so – why not? I guess he was looking for a place to put her. And her pack. He still had that.'

'In a swamp?' Dickie said.

'Yeah. In a swamp. Then he spent the night, or was it two? The motel had the records. If they'd found the body sooner, he was gone. But he drove back to Whangarei, he sold his car and got his story straight if he needed it, and that's where it is. He's not short of something up here.' Tom tapped his head.

'What about—' Dickie began, but Cheryl broke in: 'Dad, I don't want to hear any more. I want to have a walk on the beach and get some air.'

'Good idea,' Tom said.

Dickie was keen to join them, but I changed into slacks to give them a start. He walked beside me, grumbling.

'I like Tom,' I said, trying to wipe out all I'd heard of Buckley.

'He's not a bad bloke for a copper,' Dickie replied.

He cheered up when a girl in a white bathing suit ran up from the sea and vanished into the dark.

'An apparition. A white rose,' Dickie said. He's getting quite good with words.

❀ ❀ ❀

IT'S LOVELY AUTUMN WEATHER. DICKIE IS PRUNING WHILE I, murmuring 'Sorry', neglect my cactuses. He's more sensible this year, wearing gloves, but still he gets scratches on his wrists. He licks the blood away with a kind of relish. I try to hold him as a talisman, but can't bring him into the centre of my mind where I'll find a grasp. Dickie exists in the realm of certainty, and certainty for the moment is abolished. In my new reality there's only intuitive knowledge . . .

Which is never wrong. There's a path that turns aside and leads you miles and miles, while consciousness blinks and time makes a pause, until you're back in your starting place, where everything has changed its shape . . .

I knew at Lionel's gate that the car belonged to Buckley – the way it sat there as if by right. I've always liked VWs in spite of their Nazi associations. A people's car is a nice idea. This was the early sort, before they grew fat. It was the dark green of creek-weed growing on rocks, and had an old white-on-black number plate, LK something, and tyres like a bald head, and half-moons in the dust on its front window. It had a little cross on a plastic chain hanging from its rear-vision mirror, and a gaping pizza box on the passenger seat, with crusts in a pile against the hinge.

Fifty, sixty, more than sixty years ago, Clyde had leaned his balloon-tyred bike on our letterbox. What detail signalled the continuity? One front tyre mounted on the footpath, was that it? The bonnet rounded like his tennis-ball head? Or was it simply that I'd spoken his name to Tom. I'd rubbed the lamp and let the genie out, and it was time for him to park his car at Lionel's gate?

I ran up the steps but shifted to the lawn as I went by Lionel's bedroom. The blinds were down, as always, and the latches closed, but I wanted no whisper of me to reach Clyde Buckley. I felt he would put his hand out through the wall and hold me by the back of my neck. The chattering sound on the back lawn was Roly going back and forth with his hand mower.

'Roly,' I hissed (no, you can't hiss a word with no sibilant). 'Roly,' I blurted, running at him, 'is that Clyde Buckley's car?'

'Yeah, that's him.' He unhooked the catcher and carried grass to the compost bin.

I ran after him. 'What's he doing here? When did he come?'

'Came yesterday. Now he's back again. He's visiting.'

'What's he want? Why did you let him in?'

Roly emptied the grass clippings and spread them with his hand. He pushed his hat back on his head and rubbed his brow. I saw how old he was for the first time – saw it because he was tired.

'I didn't. I made him wait while I asked Lionel. But the bugger – sorry, Rowan – he followed me. He was right behind me when I went in. I didn't hear.'

'What did Lionel do?'

'He didn't see. Not until Clyde went past and stood by the bed. Then he just said, "Hello, Clyde." You know what Buckley did? He bent down and kissed him on the forehead.'

'No.'

'He did. Then he sat down and held Lionel's hand.'

'You let him do that?'

'How could I stop him? Anyway, Lionel wasn't worried. He liked it.'

'He couldn't have . . . What did they say?'

'Nothing. Clyde just sat.'

'That must be wrong. There's got to be more. You didn't see?'

'No, I didn't, 'cause I got out. They've probably said a lot by now. Yeah.'

'How long did he stay?'

'About an hour. That was yesterday. Now he's back. Look, Rowan, Lionel's OK. He even got up last night. He walked around the house. You could see it was hurting him, that thing he's got . . .'

'Polymyalgia.'

'Yeah. But he came right out to the kitchen. He said it was time we cleaned the place up. Like he was telling me to get it done.'

'And will you?'

'If that's what he wants.' Roly gave a grin. 'Then he went back to bed.'

'And Clyde Buckley came back today?'

'Half an hour ago. He brought a packet of donuts.'

'I'm going in.'

'No, don't. Rowan, he likes it. Lionel, I mean. Buckley's started something going in him.'

'Started what?'

'I don't know. But he's not here long. He's only visiting. Lionel's all right.'

'How do you know? Buckley could be doing something to him right now.'

'No, I'm watching. I won't let anything happen to Lionel. He looked after me when we were kids and it's my turn now.'

'He didn't look after you.'

'Yes he did. You don't know. He stopped big kids picking on me. And you know that time at the Catholic school, when he wrecked it?'

'Yes,' I said.

'I was there. Lionel never told anyone. He took the blame himself. But I got the spade for him when he smashed the window. I was too small to climb in, so I stayed outside and pulled plants out of the garden. There was a brand-new bed of primulas. I pulled them out and Lionel never said.'

I didn't know what to say, but knew what to do. 'I'm going in.'

I moved too quickly for him – across the lawn, on to the porch, into the kitchen, where a laugh from Lionel's bedroom stopped me in my tracks. There's a braying laugh, a whooping laugh, a chattering laugh, a splashing laugh, many sorts, but I never would have thought a weeping laugh: weeping as though with relief. Clyde Buckley was so dominant in my mind I expected him, and the sound of him, to fill the house, but this was Lionel. Lionel laughing. Then I heard his accompaniment: a series of barks from Buckley, like a dog chained to a shed at the back of a yard. I waited a moment, wanting to know what amused them, but all I heard when they stopped was a creaking chair. So I pulled myself together, pulled my right to possession of my brother tight around me, and went under the drooping lintel into the living room – my living room, Lionel's – and across the booby-trapped carpet to the bedroom door, where I looked in and saw Clyde Buckley. Saw him in profile, sitting flat-buttocked on the bedside chair.

Although I had moved quietly he knew at once I was there. He put his hands on his knees and levered himself around.

'Excuse me for not getting up, Rowan. My joints are stiff.'

It's easy to write a description suggesting that someone has an unclean spirit. I want to do it. Another part of me wants to leave him undescribed. It's superstitious, but writing him down confers power on him. Perhaps later. For now I'll just say what we said and did.

His baseball cap was on the bed. He picked it up and fitted it on his head, then raised it to me like a gentleman. It was meant to be comical. His smile was yellow (I'll allow myself that much), his voice ordinary (not unclean) as he said, 'It's nice to see you, Rowan. You're looking well. But goodness me, where's all your lovely red hair gone?'

It was hard not to respond. I opened my mouth, almost let words out, then stopped myself and ran my eyes past him.

'Lionel, are you all right?'

'Of course he is,' Clyde Buckley said. 'I reckon he's malingering. Lionel, eh, you're coming for a drive with me, old mate.'

'No he's not,' I said.

'Hey, Rowan. Just down into town to see the shops. I'll bring him back.'

'Lionel's not well. It hurts him when he gets out of bed.'

'Everything hurts when you're growing old. Look at me.' He patted his hip. 'Tin hip, this one. And see this finger?' He held it out. 'When I bend it, it locks, I can't straighten it out.' He curled it – his right index finger – and it stayed that way and seemed to beckon me. He raised the hand and peered through the aperture made by finger and thumb. We looked at each other through a tunnel of years. Then he pulled it straight with a little click. 'Trigger finger it's called, like the Wild West. But sure, it hurts. There's not much doesn't. We've got to keep on smiling, Rowan, or what's the point? Old Lionel here, me old mate, he tells me he's been stuck in bed since last winter.'

'It's his choice,' I said.

'Sure, his choice. Now what's wrong with me giving him a little treat? Downtown to look at the shops. I tell you, this town has changed. Where's all the places we used to go? Where's Cascade Park, eh? How about we see if we can find it and jag some sprats. You can come too, Rowan. Make up for that dance I asked you for, when you turned me down.'

He was going everywhere, I couldn't keep track, and Lionel lay propped in his pillows listening – listening, it seemed, with his eyes, they were so bright.

I said, 'You can talk to Lionel as long as you like, but I'm not letting you take him anywhere.'

Clyde Buckley pulled his eyes off me – they stayed genial by some long-learned trick – turned them to Lionel and said, 'It looks like Rowan rules the roost. She always was the ginger girl.'

'Mind your business, Rowan. You've never offered to take me,' Lionel said.

'I try to get you out of bed every time I come.'

Clyde Buckley grinned. 'Not hard enough, eh? It takes an old mate. Where's your grundies, Lionel? Can't take you in your PJs. Where are they, Rowan? Then you can toddle off while I dress him. An old man is not a pretty sight.'

'There's stuff in one of those drawers,' Lionel said.

'Lionel, listen to me,' I said. 'You can't let someone just walk in and take over your house –'

'Not doing that,' Clyde Buckley said.

'– as though he owns it, and owns you. You've got Roly out there and you've got me. We're the ones who care about you, no one else. And this man –' I looked at him and looked away '– what does he want? What's he after? Do you know about him? Do you know?'

'Now what's to know, Rowan?' Buckley said; and now there was a change in him, as though he had compacted himself and changed his skin to a chitinous shell – and, saying that, I feel I'm playing his game. 'I've lived a quiet life,' he went on. 'I've never spent a day inside, if that's what you mean.'

'We've heard all about you.'

He gave a sharp denying nod. 'Shouldn't listen to gossip. Shouldn't listen to lies.'

'The police don't think it's lies.'

But suddenly I was adrift, for after all, what did I know? I felt as if I'd stepped inside with him, out of my life into his, and he had put his hand on me and eased me to a place where he could find me when he wanted.

'Anyway . . .'

I was floundering and could see no way to turn. Something moved in me like a chemical change, solid into liquid, into gas, and carried away any comprehension I could have that the person sitting only a finger's touch away was a murderer.

'Anyway, Lionel's not well enough. He can't go,' I whispered.

Buckley wouldn't let me get away. 'Rowan, that poor little girl's not down to me.'

'So you know about her?'

'Stop it, Rowan,' Lionel said.

'No, let her go. I'm used to it. The cops have been dragging me in for twenty-five years. How would you like that? Police on your doorstep for something you never did. Not nice, Rowan. But sure, I know about her, the poor girl. But I never did it. Cross my heart.'

He drew his forefinger one way then the other across his chest, as we had done when we were children. It brought him back – *that* Clyde Buckley – and allowed me to break free from him. I knew he had murdered the girl.

'Lionel –'

'Go away, Rowan. I want to get dressed.'

I almost ran. I tripped on a loop in the carpet, I jarred my shoulder on the door-frame; and, outside, I lunged at Roly, who was standing up from wiping the mower blades, and held him by the biceps, digging my fingers in.

'Roly, he did it. He killed that girl.'

'Did he say that?'

'No, he didn't. But I know. And Cheryl's friend was in the police. They know he did.'

'Take it easy, Rowan –'

'He's taking Lionel. Why does he want Lionel?'

'Listen, Rowan. Sit down.' He took me to the chair by the old dunny. 'Now calm down. He can't hurt Lionel. And Lionel wasn't in it with him, if that's what you think. Lionel was in Christchurch. That's for sure, Rowan.'

'I know. I know. But why's he come now? What does he want?'

'Maybe he's just a poor lonely old bugger. And maybe he's sorry.'

'No he's not. Not Clyde Buckley.' Something was wriggling in me like a maggot. It showed its head and I had it: Buckley's phrase 'poor little girl'. He'd spoken it with enjoyment. He had tasted her again.

I started to cry. It was the only relief I could find, but no real relief, for my tears were horrified and full of hate.

'We've got to stop him,' I sobbed.

Roly sat beside me and pulled one of my hands against his thigh so he could hold it. Soon Clyde Buckley and Lionel came out of the house. Lionel was wearing a suit and tie, which Buckley must have helped him with. He looked as if he was starting off on a long trip, except that his face was sick, a dying man's face. His neck was loose inside the buttoned collar. I saw him magnified as I ran across the lawn. He raised his hand.

'Go away, Rowan.'

'Whoopsie, Rowan, watch that step. You'll skin your pretty

knees,' Clyde Buckley said.

I had, in fact, stumbled and was forced to grab hydrangea stems to right myself. Roly came to my side and put his arm around me, not to hold me steady but to hold me back.

'Let him go, Rowan.'

So I stood with my younger brother and watched my lost older brother proceed down the path with his childhood friend, who was helpful with his long arms, and solicitous at the car, and easy on the accelerator as they drove away. Access Road was empty. It was as if Clyde Buckley had swept life out of it.

'Go home, Rowan. I'll phone you when they come back,' Roly said.

I went, not because I wanted to but because I could see he did not want tears and memories and conversation but needed to be alone in his garden with his plants. I drove home and had his call almost as soon as I arrived. Buckley and Lionel had stayed away for half an hour, then Buckley had helped his 'old mate' back up the path and undressed him and put him to bed. Then he'd gone, not bothering Roly with more than a wave. Lionel was sleeping.

Dickie came home, a little drunk, to be sure, and helped smooth my worries (they're more than worries) away. Dickie is my antidote to darkness. But it's more than darkness, isn't it?

THREE DAYS HAVE PASSED. CLYDE BUCKLEY HAS NOT been back. I'll still not write down what he looks like, for fear of bringing him into Access Road again.

eleven

IT'S TOO COLD FOR DICKIE TO SWIM ANY MORE. INSTEAD he walks with me, sometimes on the beach, sometimes into town. Yesterday we visited his doctor, but as Dickie won't let me come into the surgery and finds it impossible to remember what he calls 'medical guff', I've no idea why he's on stomach pills. 'Something about my gullet maybe pressing on something else.' Judging from the way he pushed the pull door going out (even though it's named) and on the walk home kicked, in order, a beer can, a cigarette packet and a bottle top, he takes his new prescription for a guarantee of health.

The bottle top pleased him especially, ricocheting from a shop front and skittering into the gutter. 'Yes!' he exclaimed. If he'd been a boxer he'd have raised his hands above his head and danced around the ring.

I've told him about Clyde Buckley and it makes him thoughtful. 'If you want me to fix him,' he says, although without his usual bravado. He agrees that something sinister is going on, some dirty play at the bottom of a ruck. 'It sounds like he's got poor old Lionel by the balls.' But oh, it's worse than that: by some corner of his soul. Yet Buckley has gone – I won't say home: can a man like that have a home? – puttering up the narrow road to Whangarei, where I pray that illness of some sort will overtake him. Where I hope – I don't really pray about anything – that death will find him. He seems so strong, though, coarse-fibredly strong.

Now I'll try to say what Buckley looks like, and not believe he'll pick up my shiver and start back to Auckland in his green VW. He's no sensitive, that is plain, yet is somehow sensitive to Lionel – and Lionel to him – by more than an accident of juvenile proximity. What happened, I think, is this: Lionel was a clever small boy, and open to excitement and whatever was new, and open to beauty as well (as most children are). He had his antennae extended into territory where they might have found anything, but found Clyde Buckley. And what was Buckley – where was he pointing? He is an equal mystery. But here I go with my description. I'll try not to confound physical with moral ugliness.

Several times I've mentioned his long arms. It suggests something ape-like. That's mistaken. It's bigness rather than length that takes one's notice – it's heaviness and muscularity, even though there must be old-age wasting inside his sleeves. Heavy hands; flat fingernails as yellow as cow horn. The pot belly that Tom says features in police files is certainly on show but seems to come from slippage rather than growth. It houses – and this is hysterical, yet it's how I feel – yards and yards of intestine, doubling back, and gives the impression that hunger and its satisfactions predominate in the man, which is why it's legitimate for me to mention it. When he takes off his silly cap (the sort youngsters wear back-to-front), his hair is thin, his scalp is white. There are blackheads in his crinkled forehead; there are flakes of dry skin in his eyebrow roots. Nose fat and rounded, and sloping to a point, like the nose of his VW car. Wet mouth. (As a child his lips were sticky. They made a popping sound when he freed them from each other.) I've mentioned his round head, his tennis-ball head. That has a neat sound; but the sections don't meet properly, they're ridged along the joint, just as all the features I've described are loose from each other and don't seem anchored to the bones underneath. His teeth are yellow – although most old people's are like that, my dentist has a struggle to keep mine white. He pretends to manners – lifted his cap to me, as I've described – but dug a fragment of pizza meat from his gums and studied it on his fingernail before licking it into his mouth.

This is just a collection of bits, all seen with a prejudiced eye, and with anyone else it's unfair; but his failure in holding together expresses him. Clyde Buckley was never finished. Some infection got in and stopped the bonding of his parts and stopped his bonding with the rest of us.

I haven't mentioned his eyes. Small, blue, bright, amused and human. That is a terrible thing about Clyde Buckley.

I DREAM A LOT BUT USUALLY FORGET MY DREAMS when I wake. They're stories, I remember that much, and I'm always the main character, although I'm sometimes in someone else's skin. I try hard to remember because, except for anxiety dreams, I often wake satisfied, but the narrative thins like wispy clouds in the sky. It dissolves and never comes back. Yet I'm happy all morning because of my dreams.

Last night I had a different sort. It won't go away. It's like the shadow that invades the eye as people go blind.

I was walking on a bare path worn in grass. Little muddy pools wet my feet. It was night, no moon, no stars, yet I could see my white hands lighting the way. I was afraid. Darkness and silence wrapped me like a wet cloth. Then, distantly, I heard footsteps padding behind me. I did not look round but started to run. The footsteps ran soft and heavy on the sodden ground. They came closer, until I did not know whether the sounds I heard were feet or breathing. Yet the thing could not see me; it followed the rag of fear I left behind. I saw a little side path plunging down. Banks of wet clay rose on either side. I ran down a short way, then sank on my knees to listen. The footsteps stopped. The breathing kept on. Then the thing, the creature, turned its head – a head I could not see, and the body a non-shape, blotting the night. It looked down the path and grunted, and followed me. I ran. It came closer. I scrambled up the clay bank. On top were swathes of cut scrub. I lay down and pulled them over me and stopped my breathing. The footsteps approached on the path, thumping like a drum. At the bottom of the bank they fell silent. The creature looked around and sniffed. I heard him sniff. Then he took two steps – only two – up the bank. He leaned over me and pulled the scrub away . . .

I never saw him. Before I could see, I woke up.

Dickie had turned on his lamp. He scrambled from his bed and leaned over me. 'Boatie, what's wrong? Are you all right?'

'Dream,' I gasped. 'Oh God, he nearly got me.' I turned my face against his chest.

'There, there,' he said. I never thought I'd hear those words. 'It's Dickie, love. It's only me.'

Later he brought me a glass of whisky and made me drink the foul stuff neat. He had one himself to keep me company. We talked for a while, and I asked him why I remembered this dream when all my others faded as I woke.

'Comes off a different level,' Dickie said.

But my explanation is that it's a Buckley dream. It means Clyde Buckley isn't finished with us yet.

* * *

I HATE GOING THERE BUT I DRIVE OVER ONCE A WEEK.
Although Lionel has gone back to his invalid state, he's more
lively in the part of his mind that turns my questions aside.
Sometimes he answers as though for his own information,
as though his voice buzzes and prickles inside his head. For
the rest of it, when I talk of cups of tea and clean sheets,
he's simply deaf. I wonder if he knows any more what clean
sheets are.

I wash them all the same in the machine the previous
owner left in the wash-house. It's an old paddle beater that
reminds me of passing time. The rhythm is like footsteps
and the creaking wringer like a door. I peg out sheets and
pillow slips, shirts, socks, singlets, underpants – I'm Roly's
charwoman too – the way my mother used to, but instead of
wooden pegs mine are plastic, purple and green. (The world
moves on.) I don't do ironing, what's the point? The house,
inside and out, is creased and clogged, it's hairy with dust,
and why introduce ironed sheets into that squalor? Folding is
enough. Roly's bedroom has a semblance of order – clothes
on a chair, not on the floor – and he's made an effort in the
scullery, but the kitchen and living room remain little better
than corridors through junk. I tidy Lionel's bedroom as far as
I can. I pull back his curtains and sweep the floor, where last
week I found evidence of mice. I told Roly, and he says he'll

set a trap, but I know he won't. He's ruthless with slugs and snails in the garden, but mice are warm-blooded which places them on the human side of nature's divide. (I think that's how his mind would work if he thought about it.) I've seen cats skulking at the back door. Perhaps they come inside, though I haven't found any chewed mice yet.

When I get home I take a shower and walk on the beach to breathe clean air.

I can't understand Roly. Is he starting to sink along with Lionel? Or perhaps it is just that the garden is his house. I can understand him choosing to live there. Clean earth, moving air, plants feasting on the sun, and all the invisible connections he feels in his body and mind. But why can't he extend himself more in the living room and kitchen? Perhaps his spirit hibernates, falls into some sort of dusty unnatural sleep when each night he comes in from his world outside. I ask him what he and Lionel talk about.

'Nothing much.'

I ask if Lionel talks about Clyde Buckley.

'I haven't said any stuff about him. Buckley's gone.'

Yes, Buckley has removed himself, his long arms and pot belly, his yellow grin and the Adam's apple that rose and fell like a stopcock in his throat, but has left himself behind by his act of dominance. He keeps a miasmic presence in Lionel's room. More than that, he sits in the bedside chair, he holds Lionel's hand, and I can't push him out. Clyde Buckley lives with Lionel now.

Even worse, he rides home with me. How I cling to Dickie. He feels it, he likes it, but it worries him. He believes my mind is too much at work (he has always been suspicious of mind) and if I'm not careful I'll get sick. He has a horror of 'sick in the head'.

Yesterday Cheryl's attacker came up in court and the judge remanded him for a psychiatric report. Dickie is furious. The process is likely to take months. Cheryl only hopes they'll find some way to help the boy. How did we have such a pleasant child? I hope so too, but at times I'm savage to have him locked away, and this is mixed up with Buckley. The truth is that when I say I want Buckley gone, I want him dead, because I think his influence is as strong as life. All day long I invent metaphors: the name Buckley written on a blackboard and my hand with a damp cloth wiping the board clean; Roly in the garden treading a snail under his boot – that sort of thing. It's a kind of sickness, and I daren't let Dickie know.

To keep myself busy I'm getting my neglected cactuses in shape. With autumn closing down, there is not much to do. Many of them need re-potting, which I don't enjoy. I think I'll get rid of them soon. I feel the need for something simpler to look after, and simpler in their natures and more at home with my mind that doesn't want to produce prickly little bunched fists and unlikely flowers. I'll get Griff in to dig some beds, but have no ambition beyond primulas and impatiens, with perhaps some stock and wallflowers for their scent. Dickie will want to grab my cactus space for a barbecue stove, but if that happens I'll tell him I've decided to grow orchids there. The thought of orchids moves me miles away from Clyde Buckley, yet like a stream of dirty water he trickles back by roundabout ways.

Reading gets rid of him for a while. I revisit some of my favourite poems:

Grow old along with me, the best is yet to be . . .

Snippets float up in my memory:

. . . the moving waters at their priest-like task . . .
. . . a slumber did my spirit steal . . .
. . . gather ye rose-buds while ye may . . .

I've enjoyed them for years, renewable sweets I suck to remind myself that disappointments pass and beauty remains. They don't keep Buckley out for long. Nor does Georgette Heyer. Once she was my guilty pleasure. Now she's my solace and delight. I step inside her world and close the door – close it on disbelief and political conviction – and live in that free-floating world of masks and duels and gaming tables and coaches and highwaymen. Suspended disbelief, that's the thing. Suspended judgement, suspended good sense, outrage put to sleep by story-telling. The farm workers (out of the picture) are starving in hovels on the estates of the charming wastrels rolling dice at the gaming tables in Whites and the silly heiresses dressing for the ball. I don't care. The peasants can go hang for a little while. The next turn of the plot engages me . . .

But nothing, nothing, keeps Clyde Buckley away.

. . . the sedge is withered from the lake,
And no birds sing.

❋ ❋ ❋

CLOUDS HUNG THEIR BELLIES OVER THE SEA. THE WATER
was leaden and the waves slid up the sand like oil. I beat the rain
home by several minutes but couldn't keep it out of the house.
The sound on the iron roof was like a train in a tunnel.

The telephone rang and Roly's voice came winding and
crackling along the wire. He sounded old; he sounded a hundred years ago.

'Rowan, there's thunder and lightning over here. You'd better not come.'

'Why not? It's my day.'

'There's water running down the front steps. The roof's
got a leak.'

'Which room?'

'Eh? The kitchen. It's all right. I've put a bucket under it.'

'Get it fixed, Roly. I'll pay.'

'OK. But you'd better stay home. It's hailing now.' His voice
was lost in the roar. Then he said sadly, 'My garden will be getting knocked to bits.'

'I'm coming over. Is there any shopping you want done on
the way?'

'I did the shopping. You'll never get out of the car. You'll get soaked.'

'What's wrong, Roly? Why are you stopping me?'

'I'm not stopping you. There's just no need. Lionel won't talk to you. He won't talk to me –'

'Something's happened, hasn't it? Tell me, quick.'

'No, nothing's happened. I've got to go now. There's another leak . . .' And he hung up.

I knew it was Buckley. He had infected us like a disease. There was no getting well from him.

I drove through the storm with the car lights on, the wipers at high speed and the wheels surfing water over the footpaths. As I came into Loomis, the rain stopped and the sky turned blue. It was one of those hour-long Auckland storms that send down buckets of rain and truckloads of hail and then hurry away as though it's all been a mistake. The gutters were running brown in Access Road but the asphalt was clean. Half an hour would have the surface steaming.

I went into the hollow by the culvert and up the other side to Lionel's house – our parents' house, my house – expecting to find Clyde Buckley's car at the gate. No car was there. A trickle of water ran down a new channel carved by the rain beside the steps. That clay, that yellow clay, was the clay of my childhood. I almost wept at the sight of it.

twelve

ROLY WAS AT THE KITCHEN TABLE, READING THE MORNING paper. With rubbish piled around him, with wire-rimmed glasses on his nose and a bucket on the table catching drips from the ceiling, he looked like a character in a TV adaptation of a Dickens novel.

'You didn't need to come, Rowan. There's nothing you can do.'

'He's been here, hasn't he? Clyde Buckley?'

'Not for long, Rowan. He didn't stay long. He's gone back home.'

'When was he here?'

'Lunchtime. There's no harm. He just sat with Lionel for a while. Then he went away.'

'Back to Whangarei?'

'That's what he said.'

'How's Lionel?'

'Sleeping, I think.'

I pulled out a chair and sat down. My heart was thumping as it does in the night when I wake to hear a burglar coughing by the bedroom door. It takes a moment to understand that in the still of 2 a.m. it's someone passing on the footpath outside. I quietened down. Buckley had gone. But why had he been here, what did he want?

'How do you know he's gone back home?'

'That's what he said. Back to the winterless north, he said. He left some jam donuts. I threw them out.'

'Did he say anything else?'

'No, just, "Old Lionel, he's a character", that's all.'

'What did he mean?'

'I don't know, Rowan. Things don't always have to mean stuff.'

'They do. They do. If he comes again, call the police.'

Roly smacked his hand on the table. 'And tell them what? For God's sake, Rowan . . .' He couldn't go on.

'Say what you want to, Roly.'

'Buckley can't do us any harm. He's just being friendly. Maybe he's lonely. God knows, he was lonely when he was a kid.'

'Yes? So he cut the heads off baby birds.'

'Ah, Rowan.'

'And why did you throw his donuts away?'

'I don't . . .'

'Don't what?'

'I don't like sweet stuff.'

'Oh, Roly.' I took his hand. Tears were wetting my cheeks. 'Look what he's doing to us.'

'He's gone now. I really think he's gone.'

'He'll never go.' I released his hand and stood up. 'I'm going to see Lionel. What will you do?'

'I don't know. I've looked at the garden. There's nothing I can do until it dries out. I'll go on the roof.'

'Don't fall off.'

'It's rusting through, Rowan. We need a new roof.'

'I know, I know.' I took out my tissues and dried my eyes. 'Let me choose the colour.'

I went through the living room into Lionel's bedroom. He had pulled his bedclothes under his chin, then freed his arms on the blanket, where his hands lay on their backs with the fingers curled like bird claws. His head was turned not towards the wall in his usual way but towards the door, exposing one white porcelain ear – a fine ear, I thought, a gentleman's ear. It was out of keeping with his forehead and cheeks, which had their usual soreness. Yet I sensed a change in him. How was it that I knew Lionel was happy at last?

I stopped halfway between the bed and the door. Buckley's

chair stood on an angle where he had pushed it. Its hard little cushion carried the dent of his behind. It was as if Lionel had made a sigh and cancelled the man. This reading came written in the air, out of our past, out of Lionel and me and our difference. In spite of my dissatisfactions and frequent melancholy, brought on by language as often as not, I live in a happy world. Lionel entered the world of the unhappy through an agency outside himself and, I suppose, through readiness and susceptibility. He had no need, no deep need, to reside there. Until the end, he made no great struggle to get out. Yet he had done it. Standing by the bedroom door, I knew.

'Lionel,' I whispered, and when he did not wake, would have crept away. But the basement door opened and Roly dragged the ladder out directly beneath Lionel's head. He gave a cough and clenched his hands and opened his eyes.

I pushed Buckley's cushion off the chair and sat down. I said hello as though to a man I'd never met.

Lionel blinked at me. It took him a moment to know who I was. Then I saw from the stretching of his lips that I was welcome. It was less a smile than the acceptance of what he had done and where he must go; and at once I was avid to know the before of it, how he had got to this point.

'Lionel?' I said – no more than that.

'Thought you'd come. You can smell old Clyde, can't you?' His voice was creaky and needed oiling. His eyes were out of practice in resting on a face.

'I know he's been.'

'Yes, he's been. What's that noise?'

'It's Roly with the ladder. He's going on the roof.'

'What for?'

'There's a leak in the kitchen. Didn't you hear the storm?'

'I thought it was the world turning over.' Lionel made a sound I can only call a snigger. He was tasting and swallowing self-satisfaction. But it was no more than a passing busyness in his mind. Deeper, he was happy. And deeper again, horrified still.

'There was hail,' I said. 'I could hardly drive in it.'

'I wonder if it caught Clyde? Are there any of those donuts left?'

'Roly threw them out.'

A spasm of anger crossed Lionel's face. 'They were mine.'

'I'll make you some tea soon. I'll make some toast.' I was desperate to keep him open, keep him talking. One wrong word would close him down. 'Lionel,' I said, 'has he really gone back to Whangarei or is he –' I could not find the proper word '– waiting around?'

Lionel ran the white edge of his tongue over his lips, tasting donuts perhaps. He turned his head away, denying me as he had for years, and I could think of no way of bringing him back, so made a wild throw with his own words.

'You were right, I can smell him. I smell him in this room.' Then I added something of my own: 'He's like a swamp.'

Lionel rolled his head back and looked at me. His eyes held a gleam of interest.

'If you think you know what Clyde's like, you're wrong.'

'What is he like? You can tell me.'

'Do you want to know? I don't think you do. What you want to know is what I'm like.'

This was my brother lying in the bed – a strange old man I knew almost nothing of, yet knew deeply by means of love. I could not make out what that love was anchored on.

'Yes,' I said, 'I want to know that.'

'You're nosy, aren't you, Rowan? You always wanted to see. You got some frights, eh, poking around?'

'I saw some things,' I said.

'You didn't see enough.'

I had known that for a long time. 'Tell me,' I said.

Lionel stayed silent. His eyes made a number of slow blinks, as if he was considering and saying no, and moving on and saying no again. He seemed to draw away from me a little more each time and close himself into his long silence and refusal.

I became afraid of losing him, and said, 'Clyde killed a girl. The police know that. They just haven't got enough evidence.'

He looked at me in a passive way, as if what I had said was a fact as simple as breathing. 'A girl hitch-hiking,' he said.

'Has he told you he did it?'

'Doesn't have to. Everyone knows.'

'Has he talked about it with you? Is that what's wrong?'

'Wrong?' he said.

'Why you're like this, Lionel. Why you've given your life away.'

'That's a dumb way of putting it.'

'It's true, isn't it? Lying in bed like this. How many years? If that's not giving your life away . . . But something's happened, hasn't it? Something with Clyde.'

Lionel smiled at me. 'It's been good to see him,' he said.

'Lionel, tell me. It's my business. You're my brother, and I love you and I can't stand seeing you like this. He got hold of you. He twisted you round. He spoiled your life. You can tell me, and we'll stop him coming here.'

'You're a silly girl, Rowan,' he said.

That seemed true. I was breaking so feebly against him. Yet I was, in a way, pressed up close, and unless I could find the right words, the right question, I would slide away and we'd both be lost again.

I said, 'Were you in it with him, when he killed that girl?'

The smells in the room: the bad air his lurch of rage released from the blankets; the smell of Buckley. The sound he made was like a cat spitting. Spittle flew from his mouth. He half sat up and made a swipe at me with his further hand, but toppled as his other arm collapsed under him. He lay half on his face.

'Bitch, Rowan. Bitch. Get out of here.'

I was appalled, which made me want to run; but I was also triumphant, and that was stronger. I remember thinking, I've got you now.

I straightened him and settled him in his pillows.

'I shouldn't have asked that, Lionel. I know you weren't.'

'You don't know anything,' he panted.

We sat a while. Roly's boots bongo-drummed on the roof. He climbed to the chimney, where he whispered, 'Hello down there. This is God speaking.' One of Dad's jokes. It was like a puff of wind stirring rubbish in the next room.

Lionel did not hear. After a while he said, whispering too, 'I had nothing to do with it.'

'I know, Lionel. I'm sorry.'

'But I could have stopped him,' he said.

'How could you if you weren't there?'

'I wasn't really,' he said. 'Not really there.'

I demanded to know what he meant, thinking he'd found a drain that had to be cleaned out, some delusion rising from their days of running together.

'I was there another time,' he said.

I sat as though made of glass. A movement would run hair-line cracks through me and I'd fall to pieces. I'm not sure that my heart kept beating.

'Do you want to know about it, Rowan?'

'I'm –' I said, beginning to say that I was not sure, while *yes* and *no* darted like fish in my mind.

'I told Clyde today,' he went on.

'Told him what?' I managed to say.

'That we had to tell the police what we did.'

❄ ❄ ❄

THE FACTS AS HE WENT ON IN HIS CREAKING, PIPING voice – child and young man and dying man together – crisscrossed each other like pick-up-sticks, and the best thing for me now is to lay them in a row, everything neat.

It was the night I met Dickie Pinker. Lionel was home on holiday from dental school. Clyde picked him up in his ramshackle car and they drove to the Orange Hall in town. The dance there was 'no good', so they headed back west to the Loomis RSA hall, where Clyde spotted me and asked me to dance. Dickie told him, 'Shove off.' I saw Lionel as we left. He had peeled away from Clyde to drink beer with some friends among the parked cars.

Dickie drove me home. I'm part of the story; I put myself in, shivering as I take my place. We sat in the car outside my parents' house. Necking or petting, it was called. Next time I would 'go all the way'. How hungrily I wanted that. Down in the town, Clyde Buckley pulled Lionel away from his friends and drove up the hill and turned into Te Atatu Road. Lionel wanted to be dropped off. But Buckley saw the car in front of Mum and Dad's house, with two heads in it, glued together. He swung his car in a U-turn and headed through the suburbs towards Auckland, hunting now. Clyde Buckley was hunting.

The speedway races were over at Western Springs and the crowds were gone. But driving along the road by the golf course Clyde suddenly braked and started to back.

What? Lionel asked.

Did you see her? Clyde said.

She was beside a bush with her head in her arms. When Clyde stopped the car, she raised her face and Lionel guessed she was about sixteen. He helped her into the back of Clyde's car and asked where she wanted to go. She said her friends had dumped her and she'd started walking home to Avondale.

Get in with her. You go first, Clyde said.

Lionel would not. The girl stank of vomit. She slumped across the back seat.

Clyde turned the car, but when they reached Avondale he drove straight through. The girl was asleep.

I know a good place, Clyde said.

It was the pine reserve at the back of the Waikumete Cemetery.

She's too drunk. She doesn't know what she's doing, Lionel said.

Go for a walk, Clyde said.

Lionel walked half a mile up the gravel road and then walked back. Clyde was in the car, smoking a cigarette.

Where is she? Lionel said.

In there. He pointed at the trees.

Lionel knew then that Clyde had killed her.

She just stopped breathing, Clyde said. I guess she choked or something.

Lionel had some medical knowledge from his dental course. Clyde struck matches while he tried to revive the girl. She was limp. She was dead. Clyde had stuffed pine needles in her mouth. They grew like bristles. Lionel hooked them out.

He tried to make her look like a person again.

I was trying to keep her quiet, Clyde said.

We've got to get the police, Lionel said.

Clyde was ready for that. We both did this, you and me.

Not me, Lionel said.

Then something came boring at him, boring through the night, and he understood that what Clyde said was true.

Lionel has carried that knowledge ever since.

Here is how they got rid of the body. (But I must stop saying the body. The girl. She was Elizabeth Gillies, called Betty, who had left Avondale College only a week earlier, when she turned sixteen, and was trialling as a sales assistant in a Queen Street shoe shop.)

They lifted Elizabeth Gillies into the back seat of the car and Clyde drove to an orchard road in Oratia where a packing shed was being built. They loaded a dozen hollow-centred concrete blocks into the car boot, then Clyde scouted round and found a roll of binding twine. They drove to the end of Access Road.

'No,' I said, 'not there.'

'He was mad,' Lionel said.

Access Road was sleeping. Clyde crept his car into the hollow where the skeletons of two half-built houses stood against the sky. They dragged Elizabeth Gillies through the scrub and through the culvert, one on each arm. They pulled her down the side of the swamp until it widened into a pool. Lionel went back to the car for the concrete blocks. It took him six trips.

Clyde kept the girl in shallow water while he tied a block to each arm, then each leg. He broke the twine by sawing it on the rough edge of a block. He tied one to her chest by running twine under her armpits and round her throat. The moon went down, but Lionel said it was as though a light only they could see gathered around them. Clyde stripped to his underpants. He dragged Elizabeth Gillies into deep water, where the blocks sank her evenly like a water-logged tree trunk. He kept on diving and surfacing, and each time down there he pulled her deeper along the sloping bottom of the pool until she was, he told Lionel, ten feet down. Lionel did not think the water could be as deep as that. He does not remember Clyde swimming when they were boys. He dog-paddled at Cascade Park, churning the surface behind him with his feet, yet here he was rising, sinking in the ice-cold pool, eyes and teeth white in the starlight. Lionel handed him the remaining blocks one by one, and Clyde walked into the water, shoulders gleaming, head sinking, leaving an uprush of bubbles as he vanished. Deep in the pool, where there was a groove filled with silt, he placed the blocks on Elizabeth Gillies. Each time he came back, Lionel saw that Clyde was enjoying himself.

'He was having fun,' Lionel said.

Clyde dried himself with his shirt and singlet and pulled them on. He drove Lionel to Te Atatu Road. Before letting him out, he took his hand. Lionel could not tell whether it was a handshake or an attempt to crush him into submission. He felt his bones grate.

You and me, Lionel, Clyde said.

He pushed Lionel out and drove away.

SHE HAS LAIN THERE EVER SINCE, UNDER HER BLANKET of hollow-stone blocks. She sank deeper into the ooze and silt. Access Road was pushed through the farm to the Great North Road. Houses went up on either side. Some time in the seventies workmen drained the swamp and built a concrete channel for the stream. No one found her. She has settled as deep as it's possible to go.

Elizabeth Gillies is one of those girls who vanish. We seem to have a lot of them. Does anyone remember her or is she just a file in a storage vault somewhere?

'She's alive,' Lionel said. One of his hands rose slowly to his forehead. 'I told Clyde that. She's in here.'

Lionel says she gets more alive every day. The other girl, the hitch-hiker, Mandy Barnes, stands like a ghost at her side.

Roly climbed down from the roof and slid the ladder under the house. I waited for him to come and save me from Lionel, who might climb from his bed on stick-thin legs and crumple me in his hands like a paper bag. I shook off the feeling, and wanted to push him under the blankets and hide him from sight. He had let a girl be murdered. He had walked away up the road while it went on. So Clyde Buckley was right: it wasn't just Clyde, it was Clyde and Lionel.

I said, 'You knew he'd do something bad to her. You must have known.'

But I did not keep on and Lionel did not answer. He has held these conversations with himself for sixty years. When Buckley walked in at the end of that time and kissed him on the forehead and sat by his bed, it brought talk and questions to an end.

'What did you tell him?' I said.

'That I was thinking of telling the police.'

'Thinking?'

Lionel grinned. 'I didn't want to scare him too much.'

'What did he say?'

'He said I didn't have the guts.'

'That's all?'

'He said I was a character.'

'That's what he said to Roly.'

'And he said he was going back to Whangarei and I could stew in my own juice.'

Roly hadn't come inside and now I didn't want him. Lionel had drawn me in and I could not escape.

'Will you? Will you tell the police?'

'When I'm ready.'

'They'll put you in prison.'

'Good. That's good.'

He closed his eyes, this time not to block me out or send me away.

'Thank you for coming here, Rowan. But you shouldn't come any more. And Roly should go somewhere else.'

'Have you told Roly?'

'You're the pushy one. I'll just let him find out.'

'Listen. Listen, Lionel. Cheryl's got a friend who was a policeman. I'll ask him what you should do. He's had lots of experience—'

'No.' His eyes shot open, and he looked at me with his old anger and dislike. 'Don't interfere. This is mine. Leave it alone.'

'I just want to help.'

'No one can help.'

We sat quiet for a while. Within two minutes of learning about a murder, and my brother's part in it, I was quiet. Not at peace – how could I be? I might never be at peace again. But quiet with the ending of Lionel's long sickness and wasting away. Now we paused. But on either side of this moment Elizabeth Gillies lay dead.

'They looked for her a long time,' I said.

Lionel nodded.

'Didn't someone see her in Sydney?'

'And other places.'

'And all the time . . .'

'Be quiet, Rowan.'

I obeyed him for as long as I could.

'How did you let Clyde Buckley get hold of you like that?'

One of his hands, outside the blanket, fell on the other

and fastened there. 'I could give him hidings, then he got bigger than me. He'd do anything. I got stuck on to him and I couldn't get off.'

'Like a fly on fly paper,' I said.

Lionel gave a single laugh. 'Good enough, Rowan. But I'm off now.'

'Will he come back?'

'He's gone. There's nothing he can do.'

'When will you tell?'

'Soon. We can never fix it for . . .' He made a small gesture at Access Road, at the swamp. 'This is just to fix me and Clyde.'

I heard Roly in the scullery, boiling the kettle. In a moment he called out, 'Tea's made.'

'Don't let him come in here,' Lionel said.

'Will you be all right?'

I wanted to touch him, yet the thought made me recoil. He understood; was preternatural in his reading of me – and, from now on, of everyone and everything. He turned his head away.

'Get out now, Rowan. You've got what you came for. And keep your mouth shut, OK?'

'Yes,' I whispered. 'I will.'

And I mean it. I'll tell no one. I'll tell these white pages, that is all.

I sit in bed, propped in my pillows, and watch the words squirm along the lines. They twitch their noses like rats sniffing rotten meat. On and on they go. What more is there to find?

Dickie sleeps in his bed four feet away. His mouth is open, poor thing. He breathes stertorously. There's a good word. I could jump over to him like Lionel jumping to Roly's bed in the night. My feet would not even touch the floor.

thirteen

ONE DAY. TWO DAYS. NOTHING HAPPENS. WHEN I PICK
up my biro, my thoughts stay fixed and I can't make them
move.

Dickie knows something is wrong. 'Something' is his word. I
answer, 'No, no, Dickie. It's just everything under the sun.'
    What else can I say?

I thought: I'll try the beach. So I walked there for an hour. The beach as medicine, the cold sand on my soles when I took off my shoes, the clean sky, 'the moving waters'. It did not work. So here I am back with my white page and my crawling pen and my thoughts like dead lips after a dentist's injection.

The thing that happened? The thing that will happen? There are two banks of fog enclosing me.

Buckley grew on Lionel like a lateral. When no one pinches them off, they can grow as large as the main stem.

I telephoned Roly. He wanted to talk about his garden. There's hail damage to his vegetables. But he sees it now as nature having her say – at least I think that's what he means when he concludes: 'It's the sort of thing that happens, isn't it?' He's busy among his bruised plants all day, while Lionel lies in bed – thinking, Roly says, whatever he thinks; although once Roly saw him at the wash-house window, peering at the damaged garden.

I asked about the leaking roof. 'Yeah, we'd better get that fixed,' he answered vaguely.

He'd taken an hour off to do the shopping. 'Lionel asked me to buy some donuts,' he said.

Cheryl popped in for a cup of tea between appointments. She looks on it as proof of her professionalism that she took a buyer to see the house where she was assaulted. The hardest thing was opening the front door, but after that she led her client boldly through the rooms and made a point of praising the kitchen. When I tell Dickie he'll say, 'That's my girl.'

I asked about Tom Quinney. She said, casually, that she was still seeing him, but could not conceal her satisfaction. It makes me nervous. The phrase I would use of her is 'deeply smitten' – am I allowed? – and from there one can be deeply hurt, which she's been before. Concern for Cheryl is good for me. Outside Access Road life goes on. I tell her that I like Tom Quinney very much and that her father likes him too. She frowns at that. At her age, she's not having her parents interfering, even if it is with approval.

Let me think. Lionel never touched Elizabeth Gillies. Would he have touched her – 'touched' is not the right word, but I can't take the step to the right one – if he had been less fastidious about smells? Why did he walk away up the road? I can see it clearly: the white dust in the moonlight, the black moon-penetrated wall of trees on his left, farm paddocks on his right (I know the territory), the bare-topped hill, where he tells himself that Clyde has had long enough. I can see that far into his mind. Long enough for what? I won't go as far as I went the day Lionel confessed to me, when I knew that he knew Clyde would hurt the girl. Perhaps he didn't know. Perhaps . . .

And what will the police do? Will they rip up the concrete channel and dig deep down, and even then will they find bones? In the end will it rest on a confession, and will they conclude that Lionel is just a mad old man? A sick old man? I think when they hear Clyde Buckley's name . . .

❊ ❊ ❊

Buckley isn't finished yet. He'll come back.

fourteen

It's over. God, it's over.

That's my blood on the page.

fifteen

NOW, CAREFULLY.

White pages. Blue lines. A fat biro with the name of Cheryl's firm printed on the barrel. These and recent memory – recent, although more than a week has passed – jostle together to form a circle. There's no way out. I can move my hand, I can move my thoughts and lift myself out of the bed, my swampy bed, that I've lain in for eight days. Monday makes a new beginning. I'll close the gates on Access Road.

I sit at my desk, where Dickie brings me a cup of tea. He frowns to see me writing. I say, 'Don't stop me, Dickie. This is for you. When I'm finished I'll show you everything I've written. Now be a dear and go away.'

He brings me a rose to help me on my way. It's out of season, a crippled rose, but still beautiful. I look into it deeply. Have you ever noticed that when you peer at something, look long and longer, the ground falls away from under your feet and you can't tell whether you're rising or falling? Rising, falling, here or there . . .

A red rose, especially a crippled one, looks like blood.

NOW THEN. ON SATURDAY AFTERNOON EIGHT DAYS ago I was drinking a cup of tea, eating an almond biscuit, reading *Faro's Daughter* for forgetfulness, and admiring Deborah Grantham so much – 'chestnut hair glowing in the candlelight' – that I made little purring sounds of delight as I turned the pages . . . when the phone rang.

'Bother,' I said, then ran to it, out of Deborah's world into mine, where consequences have no soft edges.

'Hello,' I said.

'Rowan, is that you?' Clyde Buckley said.

I lost control of my bladder – just a squirt – and made a sound of terror that scurried down the wire like a rat.

'Rowan?' he said. 'It's Clyde Buckley here. Look, I'm round at Lionel's place and he's not very well. I think he's passed out. I've rung for an ambulance but I think you should get here. This is family stuff and I'll just be in the way.'

'Roly,' I gasped. 'Is Roly there?'

'No, he's not. I suppose he's gone shopping. It's only me. Old Lionel, he looks pretty bad. Can you come?'

'What hospital? Where will they take him?'

'I don't know. Depends what's wrong with him, I suppose. If it's heart . . . You'd better get here.'

'Yes, I'm coming.'

He was saying 'Good' as I hung up. I had no idea what to do next. Dickie was at his club, where he was introducing Tom Quinney. They were due back mid-afternoon – Dickie is vague about time where the club is concerned – and Cheryl was also coming in. I should have telephoned him but I could not think straight. I scrawled a note: 'Clyde Buckley rang. Lionel is ill. Please come. R.' Then I ran into three rooms before I found the car keys where Dickie had left them on the bedside table. I drove to Loomis faster than I've ever driven before and was lucky not to have an accident. (The speed camera at Avondale picked me up: I've got a ticket.)

In Access Road I crossed the stream in its concrete bed without a thought of Elizabeth Gillies. Now, though, I wonder if she's reduced to bones or if the swamp has preserved her like the bog people Dickie and I saw in Denmark. I came across a poem about them several years ago – can't remember who wrote it. There's one line, 'the mild pods of his eyelids', that stayed in my mind, and when I think of her, Elizabeth Gillies, it's attached and saves her from Clyde Buckley for a moment – mild pods – before I remember that Buckley's hands tightened round her throat like the cord that strangled Tollund man.

I'm trying not to get to him, Clyde Buckley. But here's Access Road. Lionel's house, my house.

There was no VW at the gate. I pulled up and sat for a moment, limp with relief: the ambulance had come, Lionel was safe, Buckley was gone. Then I hurried up the path, thinking Roly might be home from shopping.

'Roly,' I cried at the back door.

The house went *tick tick* like a bomb. I stood with my hand on the door-frame, looking into its ruined insides. It was – oh, give me a word – archaeological. I can, if I wish to, study it for the rest of my life; but at that moment, eight days ago, as I leaned into the kitchen, it flashed like an image on a screen, and the next image was Lionel's bedroom (how did I get there?); then the bed, with Lionel sleeping open-mouthed; then his face close up and Lionel dead. My brother dead.

I leaned over him. His wide eyes were fixed neither far off nor near, nor were they looking within. His lips were drawn back and his dry teeth gleamed.

I must have made an exclamation of shock. I have the memory of an echoless sound in the room.

Then Clyde Buckley said, 'Poor old Lionel, eh?'

He was standing between the wardrobe and the door. At first he was a man shape, hollowed out. Then he took substance: a flannel-shirted belly, a toothy face. He raised an arm and pushed the door, which went halfway (it jams, Lionel's door, it never closes). The sound it made on the floor was like a rasping cough.

Clyde Buckley said, 'It's good to see you, Rowan, but I miss your pretty hair.'

I whispered, 'I'll scream.' No rush for the door, no anger about Lionel; nothing but two useless words.

He replied by taking three steps and grasping my shoulder like a ball. His fingers dug underneath the bones. 'No you won't, Rowan, or I'll hurt you real bad.'

'What . . .?' I managed to say; and then, half crying with pain, 'What do you want?'

With looser hands, one on each shoulder, long fingers at the back, thumbs in front, he engineered me round, turned me like a craneload, and sat me on the bed, where Lionel's hip dug into my buttocks.

'But I don't want to do that. I like you too much.' He let my shoulders go.

My hand, bracing me, came down on Lionel's stomach and I pulled it away with a little screech.

'He can't hurt you. Lionel's dead, the poor old bugger,' Clyde said.

'You did it. You killed him,' I said.

'Lionel broke his promise. We shook hands on it years ago.'

'That girl. That girl you killed . . .'

'Yeah, he told you, the silly bugger. I knew that. Old Lionel and me had a talk.' One of his hands clamped my jaw, the other tapped the bridge of my nose. 'See, if you cover someone's mouth and squeeze his nose with your other hand . . . Can't talk hard enough after that. All your secrets, eh? Don't jump around. I'd never do it to you.'

'Let me go.'

'Sure. Sure. See? I wouldn't hurt you.'

I kicked myself backwards over Lionel, but by the time I'd done it Clyde had leaned across the bed. He put his hands on me and held me flat.

'Hey, that's nice, I've got you lying down.'

'Don't you touch me. Don't you dare.'

'No, I won't. I had my look a long time ago. Sixpenceworth. Remember that?'

'You killed him, didn't you? You killed Lionel.'

'Well, I couldn't let him talk, you can see that. What I've got is, you could say, a strong instinct for self-preservation. When it comes down to it –' he tapped his chest '– me first.'

'How? How did you do it?'

'Don't worry, it didn't hurt. I wouldn't make old Lionel suffer. We were mates. Which he forgot, but never mind. I just put a pillow on his face.'

'Smothered him?'

'I guess you could say.' He pulled me back, half across Lionel, and sat on the bed, jamming his hip against my side. 'It's a pretty quick way.'

'And now you're going to do it to me.'

Clyde Buckley shook his head. 'It'll be quick. I don't go in for hurting people.'

'You hurt those girls.'

'Sure, a bit. I was pretty young then and I thought . . . Don't know what I thought. But sorry, Rowan, we can't talk any more because old Roly might come home. I've got to shut him up as well. He's a tough little sod.'

'You don't – Roly doesn't know. And I won't tell. I won't. I promise, Clyde . . .'

I confess to pleading. Anyone would plead. But when he reached to free the pillow from under Lionel's head, I grabbed his arm and bit his hand. He shook me off the way you'd shake a puppy, and held me down.

'They'll get you for this. They'll see it's murder.'

'No, Rowan, there's going to be a fire. The way this place will go up, it's better than Guy Fawkes.'

'But three of us . . .'

'They'll think it was a suicide pact. Brothers and their sister, eh, all kind of screwy.'

'They'll see we're suffocated.'

'Charred corpses, Rowan. No evidence.'

He stood and pushed me flat, one hand clamping my throat, the other sliding the pillow out, which turned Lionel's head and made me think he was alive. I thrashed my legs. One of my shoes went flying and banged the wall. I looped my arm around Clyde Buckley's elbow, trying to pull his hand from my throat – and suddenly it left me, and the pillow hesitated, drooping its ears each side of my face. Clyde Buckley half turned, half rose from his crouch, swivelled his head and seemed to listen with his side-twisted mouth.

'Shit,' he said.

Would I have thought of Dickie as I died? Probably not. I don't think you do. Nor did I think of him arriving in time to stop Clyde Buckley; but now, reconstructing, I give myself licence to put things in – and I knew in my fibres that Dickie would come. It's of a piece with our lives. I heard feet running on the path. Clyde Buckley made a wolfish bark. His head slewed towards me with red movements in his eyes. He swung his arm and caught me with a back-handed blow on the side of my head, stunning me; so there are things I never saw and I have to sit still and collect myself, reconstruct what Dickie and Roly have told me, put it all together and try not to invent . . .

TOM QUINNEY ENJOYED HIS TIME AT THE CLUB BUT wanted to be at our house when Cheryl arrived. He and Dickie ambled down the street and missed me driving away by a minute or two. Tom's car was parked at our gate and he fingered the scrape I'd made on his rear mudguard as I left. Dickie was puzzled by the empty garage and open front door. He found my note in our message place, the corner shelf on the landing where he'd bounced into the cactus garden. After reading it he pushed it at Tom, who, I have to say, showed none of the instincts of a policeman. Dickie wasted no time arguing. He borrowed Tom's car and set off for Access Road.

Tom and Cheryl would follow in Cheryl's car.

So we drove, my husband and I, with a gap of five minutes between us, and I can't understand why the speed camera that picked me up didn't get him. This is what Dickie knew: Clyde Buckley was going to kill me unless he got to Loomis in time. ('By God, he's going to murder her,' he said to Tom, knowledge that came like a voice counting off a fact, and Tom replied, 'Hey, come on, he's an old man.' He gave Dickie his keys reluctantly – I mustn't let him or Cheryl ever read this.)

In the hollow in Access Road, Dickie passed Roly with a shopping bag in each hand. He pulled up behind our car, shunting it a little, and hurried up the path in his limping run – which I recognised the instant before Clyde Buckley struck me on the temple. Dickie reached the back door and paused. The house – I see it with his eyes – was a graveyard of dead furniture and light bulbs without shades. It made no sound and nothing moved.

'Rowan,' he called. 'Boatie.'

There was a slipping movement like a subsidence under the piles, and a contraction, a closing in – I think that's what you mean, Dickie – and I can only put it down to Clyde Buckley stepping to the bedroom door and pulling his readiness around him. A floorboard betrayed him with a BB-gun crack. Dickie moved across the kitchen to the living-room door. 'Boatie, you there?' – which I heard from a far distant place.

Clyde Buckley stepped into the red and green light. He pointed at the bedroom. 'She's having a lie-down.'

'What?' Dickie said, taking a step.

'Snoozing like a baby,' Buckley said.

He must have expected Dickie to rush past him. It would have been easy then to grab him from behind. But Dickie, nearly an All Black, thinks on his feet. He walked across the room on the slippery papers and eaten carpet, then changed direction – I've seen him do it on the field – and shoulder-charged Buckley – 'Got him in the belly where he's soft' – tumbling him across a nest of tables by the front door, where his head smashed two glass panels out of their frames. For a moment he lay helpless, with his baseball cap tipped across his face.

'I should have grabbed one of those tables and bashed him,' Dickie says. But he heard me in the silence, whimpering, and ran into the bedroom instead. Blind, dizzy, uncomprehending, I lay across Lionel. Dickie ran to the bedside. He lifted me, then saw what lay underneath. 'I nearly screamed,' he says. Blood from my face had dripped into Lionel's eyes. Dickie thought Buckley had gouged them out, and he pulled me like a grain sack over the body on to the floor, thinking only: Get away. Out of the house. He'd forgotten Buckley, who had freed himself from the smashed door and fallen tables. He met Dickie dragging me backwards into the living room and circled one thick arm around his throat, raising at the same time a banshee scream (banshee is feminine but I'll leave it in).

Dickie let me go and Buckley, shaking him left and right, pulled him to the centre of the living room. I crawled back to the bed and jerked the pull-rope of Roly's bell, which shows that I had kept a fragment of my wits. Then a thumping of heels on the floor turned me back to the living room. I saw what was happening as though through smeary glass – Buckley holding Dickie in a vice, forearm squeezing his throat, squeezing out his life. I got to my feet, and fell; crawled back through the bedroom and over the living-room carpet (felt its texture). I nipped Buckley by his trouser leg. He kicked me aside. At the same time Dickie managed to lift one foot on to the fireplace. He made a push, which threw Buckley off balance. He came down over me, his legs across my chest, with Dickie angled to one side.

We must have made a strange sight for Roly when he came in. Dickie and Buckley are almost eighty and I'm close behind, and there we lay like children wrestling on the floor. Hearing Buckley's scream – a kind of ululation – Roly had stopped halfway up the path. When the bell rang, he dropped his bags. He came through the door in time to see Buckley raise his leg and shunt me away, then straddle Dickie and try to dig his thumbs into his throat. Dickie got his arms up, he tangled hands with Buckley; and Buckley's, he says, were slabs of wood, with fingers that had an extra joint. He admits that he was done for: Buckley would have throttled him in another minute.

Roly saw it. He turned to the hearth where a loose brick from the fire surround lay in the grate. He picked it up two-handed and brought it down on the back of Buckley's head. Buckley fell forward and lay with his chest on Dickie's face.

He made some grunting noises – words he could not speak. Then slowly, slowly, he levered himself to his knees, gained his feet and walked out of the house.

Roly let him go. He knelt beside me.

I whispered, 'Lionel's dead.'

Dickie came towards me on his knees.

'Lionel's dead,' I said.

'I know, Boatie,' Dickie said. 'But you're OK.' Then he said, 'Where'd he go?' and climbed to his feet.

Banging into one wall, then the other, he followed Buckley out of the house. He says his only thought was that Buckley had gone to find a weapon.

He found him standing on the back lawn, staring into his cupped hands. His hair was black with blood, and he swayed forwards and back. Dickie ran at him – I mustn't say 'ran', all our movements were at snail's pace – and tackled him round the waist. They fell to the ground and lay side by side, Buckley on his face as though cropping the grass and Dickie looking at the sky, panting for breath.

Roly went into Lionel's bedroom and came out after a moment, pulling the door behind him until it rasped. He swept rubbish from the sofa and helped me lie down. Outside, he lifted Dickie and helped him in. He sat him on the floor beside the sofa so my arm lay over his chest. Then he rang for an ambulance and the police.

sixteen

IT'S TAKEN ME A LONG TIME TO WRITE THAT. I'VE CROSSED out all sorts of stuff, like the rope of saliva hanging from Buckley's mouth and – well, I've crossed it out. Things about Lionel. And Dickie fighting like James Bond. No need for it.

I had my stitches out yesterday. I'll have a scar running along my cheekbone. My bouts of nausea are over, but I must be careful not to get any more bangs on the head. A yellow face for me, faded from purple; and a yellow throat for Dickie, and a croaky voice. He has bruises on his arms and chest and back. It's a good thing we've both been on calcium supplements for the last few years, and eating the acidophilus Dickie loathes, or our bones would have snapped like kindling wood.

Clyde Buckley is on life support. Roly's blow broke his skull and pushed edges of bone into his parietal and occipital lobes. He kept a thread of consciousness that drew him out of the house and across the lawn towards the back of the section, where a right of way passes the Catholic school. Buckley had his beetle car parked beyond the gates.

So far no one has claimed him. Perhaps there are no Buckleys left. There's no one to say that his life support should be switched off. The doctors will decide. I hope it's soon, for everyone's sake.

We had Roly with us until the police let him move back into Access Road. I'm not sure Lionel left a will, but one way or the other Dickie and I will make sure Roly gets the house. When I mentioned it, he said, 'But half of it's yours.'

'We don't need it,' I said. 'We'll do it up for you. New paint and a new roof, all that stuff.'

'No, no –'

'Yes, Roly. Dickie and I are millionaires.'

'Are you? Good God.' He retains a 1930s view of the world and doesn't understand that little millionaires like us are a penny each.

He's back in his garden and clearing out truckloads of junk from the house. Dickie and I will drive over when we're ready and tell him how we think things should be done. Just about everything new, I suppose: wallboard and ceilings, wiring and plumbing and piles. No blue paint on the outside walls, I'll insist on that. And the rose window must stay, even though it threw its light on Clyde Buckley.

Cheryl wants to see the house and do a valuation.

No, I say, and she doesn't argue. She's moving in with Tom Quinney this weekend. Oh dear and three cheers.

The police have questioned us many times. For a while it seemed they would charge Roly with something! How absurd. I think they've let it go now. They're pleased to have the book closed on Clyde Buckley, as one of them put it, but they can't understand why he killed Lionel.

I say, It goes right back with those two. And with our family as well. My father used to chase him away, and I suppose he brooded on it and decided to get even and kill us all.

It's the best I can do.

Dickie, do you think I'm right not to tell them about Elizabeth Gillies? I don't want concrete cutters screaming over her head. I want her to lie undisturbed, with her mild pod eyelids.

We held Lionel's funeral yesterday. It was family only. Roly wants to tip the ashes in his garden. It sounds gruesome to me, but Roly says simply, I think he'd like to be there.

Dickie and I walk on the beach, hand in hand and rather slowly. Dickie is chastened. He had no idea life could be like that. (Tell me if I'm wrong, Dickie.) It's too cold for bare feet. Thin waves edge up the sand and melt away. I hunt for rhymes. Wave, cave. Sky, belie.

Find, end. That's a half-rhyme. At my age I think I'm allowed.

BLINDSIGHT

Blindsight is the story of a good though damaged man and his less than virtuous sister. As their childhood closeness unravels, Alice moves into her career in science (she's a mycologist), while Gordon descents into vagrancy and silence. For more than thirty years they do not meet. Then a young man appears at Alice's door, claiming a relationship she never knew she had. As he becomes part of her carefully guarded world, she cautiously begins to reveal the past. But is she telling him everything?

Jealousy, ambition and love shape the fates of Alice and Gordon in this compelling story of loyalty and family ties. *Blindsight* is another fine novel by the writer many acknowledge as New Zealand's best.

Winner of the Deutz Medal for Fiction, Montana Book Awards.

THE SCORNFUL MOON

Wellington, 1935, James Tinling, a former Cabinet Minister, plans a political comeback, although a brash newcomer stands in his way. James has methods of dealing with upstarts, but is handicapped by secrets in his life. Eric Clifton, world-renowned moon scientist, has secrets too. He lives hot-bloodedly and is at war with patrician James.

Sam Holloway, literary man and moralist, records their year – its sexual intrigues and sudden violence and its overturning of political norms. What role does the young poet Owen Moody play, and brothel madam Lily Maxey? There's James's daughter Charlotte too, desperately painting in a garden shed; and Sam with his dozen friends at work on a composite detective novel.

Election day. Labour wins, crushing James's party. His secrets are shockingly revealed.

IN MY FATHER'S DEN

When Celia Inverarity, aged seventeen, is found brutally murdered in a secluded West Auckland park one Sunday afternoon, Paul Prior, her English teacher and mentor, is suspected of being her murderer.

Celia's death and the violence which follows send Prior back to examine the past – which proves as secret as his father's den in the old poison shed. Eventually the murderer is exposed, but not before a family has been split again and old wounds revealed.

In My Father's Den is Maurice Gee's third novel and was first published in 1972. It is now an international feature film of the same name. *In My Father's Den* is directed by Brad McGann and produced by Trevor Haysom and Dixie Linder, and stars Matthew Macfadyen, Miranda Otto and Emily Barclay.

PLUMB TRILOGY

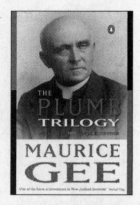

Maurice Gee's acclaimed novel *Plumb* was the winner of the Wattie Book Award and the New Zealand Fiction Award. His brilliant picture of the intolerant, irascible clergyman George Plumb has captured the New Zealand imagination.

Gee built on *Plumb's* rich possibilities with the novels *Meg* and *Sole Survivor* to set up a family trilogy unequalled in New Zealand literature.

'One of the most significant feats in New Zealand literature.' – Michael King